GREEN MOUNTAIN HERO

GREEN MOUNTAIN HERO

Written by Edgar N. Jackson
Illustrated by James O. Jackson

Based on the events in the life of
Solomon Story, eldest son of Ann Story,
known in history as "The Mother of the
Green Mountain Boys."

THE NEW ENGLAND PRESS
Shelburne, Vermont

Manufactured in the United States of America
Cover illustration by Elayne Sears
(Originally published by the Lantern Press)
First New England Press edition 1988
Second printing, November 1994
Third printing, July 1998
Fourth printing, June 2001

For additional copies of this book or for a
catalog of our other titles, please write:

The New England Press
P.O. Box 575
Shelburne, VT 05482

or e-mail nep@together.net

Visit our Web site at www.nepress.com

Jackson, Edgar Newman.
   Green Mountain Hero.

   Based on the events in the life of Solomon Story, eldest son of Ann
Story, known in history as "The mother of the Green Mountain boys."
   Reprint. Originally published : Lantern Press, 1961.
   Summary: Life is difficult for Solomon Story, his mother Ann, and
their family in pre-Revolutionary Vermont as they face the threat of
Indians and aid the Green Mountain Boys.
   1.   Vermont—History—Revolution, 1775-1783—Juvenile fic-
tion. [1. Vermont—History—Revolution, 1775-1783—Fiction. 2.
Frontier and pioneer life—Vermont—Fiction] I. Jackson, James O.,
1915-1987, ill. II. Title.
PZ7.J13244Gr 1988 [Fic] 88-31313
ISBN 0-933050-61-5

To Andy, Julie, Michael, and Courtney,
my grandchildren,
pioneers of a new generation.
May they value the pioneering spirit.

CONTENTS

GREEN
MOUNTAIN
HERO

1. HORROR IN THE NIGHT

"Wake up, wake up quick." It was Amos Story calling his children. "Solomon, Ephraim, Samuel! Get out of the house now. Don't wait. The barn is on fire, and the house may catch any minute."

Solomon was wide awake at once. He recognized the sound of alarm in his father's voice. He saw the red reflection of the dancing flames against the wall of his room.

Down the hall he heard his father calling the girls: "Hannah, Susanna, wake up, wake up." Then his mother's footsteps raced down the hallway, and Hannah and Susanna were hurried from their room.

Solomon did not have to waken Ephraim

11

or Samuel. They were quickly stirring and asking questions: "What is it? What shall we do? Shall I dress or run in my nightshirt?"

In just a few moments the family of Amos and Ann Story were out under the trees, a safe distance from the barn, watching the flames that were already racing along the edge of the roof, up toward its peak.

"What can we do, Father?" Solomon asked.

Amos barked an order at Ann: "You stay here and keep the young children away. Solomon, you come with me."

At once, Solomon followed toward the shed where the maple sap buckets were stored. Quickly, he and his father, with a bucket in each hand, drew water from the pond where the cows drank, and threw it up against the side of the house nearest the fire.

"We'll keep the end of the house soaked down," Amos yelled. "Maybe we can save it. The barn is gone, that's sure."

Solomon ran back and forth with his buckets, as did his father. Soon some neighbors, who had seen the red glow against the night sky, came galloping up on horseback. Without being told what to do, they grabbed buckets and aided in carrying water, making a

chain of men and boys from the pond to the house. Then, instead of carrying their buckets, they passed them from hand to hand.

Solomon watched large sparks as they sailed by the house. Finally, he saw a big one land on the roof. The tinder-dry shingles began to smolder.

"Father," he called, "the roof is on fire."

Instantly, his father placed a ladder against the house and was up upon the roof. The chain of men and boys passed the buckets of water up the ladder to Mr. Story, who put out the first fire and then began soaking down the roof. Here and there sparks fell, and the roof began to smolder, but always the fire was doused with water before it could make headway.

Men were commenting about the fire. Solomon tried to take in all that they were saying, but it was hard to understand some of the things.

One man said, "Amos must have put in some wet hay."

Another said, "It's a good thing it is summertime and the cows and horses are out to graze."

Said a third, "This will sure set Amos back, coming this time of year."

Solomon looked toward his mother every few minutes. She stood without moving, the younger children nearby. Ephraim was not there, and Solomon saw him in the bucket line with other men and boys. The dim light of early morning began to give an outline to things and people, so that Solomon could tell who was there and what each was doing.

The heat from the burning barn was so intense that no one could get near it. It was an old barn, fifty years or more old. The big dry timbers and the tons of hay fed the fire. Solomon could feel his face glowing with the heat, and he was more than a hundred feet from the burning barn.

"Look, the roof's going," someone yelled. Just then the big timbers of the barn roof quivered and gave way. They fell down into the burning barn, and out came a shower of great sparks that fell all over the barnyard and the house. By now, the roof of the house was well enough soaked so that the embers were quickly extinguished after landing on it.

"There goes the corncrib," called a neighbor. The small building near the barn, where Amos kept corn for chickens and pigs, burst into flames all at once, as its boards reached the kindling point.

"It's a good thing it's nearly empty now. Last year's corn is about used up, and this year's hasn't been put in yet," thought Solomon, but he didn't say anything. This was one of the times when words didn't seem to be worth much.

As morning came, the glow that had reached up to the clouds and off in all directions retreated gradually into the smoldering mass of red that was the remains of the hay so carefully stored away just a few days before.

Mrs. Perkins, the nearest neighbor, a quarter of a mile down the road, drove in with a small wagon and food for breakfast. "See here, you men," she said. "You might as well eat. There's little more you can do now, and you must all be hungry after working so hard fighting that terrible fire."

Mrs. Perkins rambled on at full speed, and the men gathered around her wagon to drink warm milk and eat corn bread and freshly browned sausage.

When the danger that the fire might spread

was over, Amos thanked the neighbors who had helped him save his home. For a while they stood around in small groups, talking about what had happened and what they could do about it.

"When you going to raise your new barn?" asked Tim Weeks, who lived up the valley. "We'll all be on hand to give you a lift." They talked of the custom of making a social event out of lifting the rafters for a new building.

"Do you think Zeke Jenny had anything to do with this?" asked Ned Walker. "He's just the kind of person to do a sneaking trick like setting a person's barn on fire."

"No," Amos Story answered. "I can't think anyone would be that mean. Really, I think it is my own fault. I was so anxious to get my hay in that I must have put in some wet grass, and that did the damage."

This puzzled Solomon. He could not see how wet grass could cause a barn to burn down. It was easier for him to think that Zeke Jenny, the Tory who had threatened his father at the town meeting, might have done it.

Feeling ran high in the town meetings between those who wanted to support their friends in Boston in fighting unfair taxes and the tea duty, and those, who were called Tories, who felt they should be loyal to the King of England, no matter what he did.

Amos Story had asked the town meeting of Salisbury, Connecticut, to offer support to their fellow colonists in Boston. Zeke Jenny said he would report Amos' treason to the colonial governor. When nearly everyone else at the town meeting supported Amos Story, Zeke became more angry than ever. When the neighbors made it uncomfortable for Zeke, he hurriedly packed and left town. It was rumored that he had gone to Vermont to work for the British, but no one knew for sure.

As the day wore on, and the danger from flying sparks or breeze-blown embers waned, most of the neighbors went home. Each expressed his regret at the damage the fire had done and offered his services to help rebuild.

Amos answered, "Thank you. We'll think about it awhile before we start to work. When we do, we'll be sure to let you know."

Quietly, Solomon watched his father from a distance. He knew how bad his father felt. He knew how hard he had worked to get the hay in. This was the first year Solomon had really been much help in the hayfields. To have all that work and hay go up in smoke tested a man's spirit.

Ephraim and Samuel, as curious small boys will do, picked at the blisters of scorched paint on the part of the house that faced the barn. Amos watched, but said nothing. He knew that part of the house would have to be painted again.

It was some time later in the day that Solomon was alone with his father. It was then that he said, "Father, how can wet hay set a barn on fire? I thought water put out a fire."

"It does sound strange, doesn't it?" Amos replied. "But I have heard of it many times. When green hay is pressed down tight, it dries out without enough air around it. This makes it hot. Sometimes it gets so hot it kindles. When that happens, the fire begins inside the barn and gets such a start that it is impossible to put it out."

Solomon was still curious: "Wouldn't it be simpler to think that somebody like Zeke Jenny set fire to the barn than to say some damp hay got hot and lit itself? I wouldn't trust Zeke Jenny after the things he said to you."

Amos smiled a bit. It was the first time Solomon had seen him smile all day. "No, I suppose you wouldn't," he said. "I don't know as I would either. But Zeke left these parts, and we know the hay was there. Because of my haste to get it in before that thunderstorm, I didn't take time to make sure it was well enough cured, and that was the cause of the fire."

Amos was not one to stand around and talk. "Come, Give me a hand. We have put off milking the cows too long. They are afraid of fire and stayed away out in the pasture, but they will be in trouble if we don't get at it soon."

It was almost the middle of the afternoon when the milking was done. As they finished, they heard the dinner bell. When they were close to the house, Ann Story called: "You men haven't had much to eat today. You'll feel better when you've had a good meal. Food is on the table. You'd better eat now."

After Amos had asked a blessing, he looked around the table at his family. Each one seemed to be expecting him to say something. Finally, after he had eaten quietly for a while, he said, "Things could be much worse. We could have lost our house and our cows and horses. We are all here, and we have a roof over our heads and enough to eat. But we'll have to do some thinking before we rebuild." And he sat there gazing out the window, with a faraway look in his eyes.

2. LEAVING HOME

It was a Sunday morning. Solomon would never forget that day. His father and mother had been talking seriously for several days, but usually when the children were not nearby. Solomon thought they were talking about the fire and rebuilding the barn. While the younger children were being dressed for church, Solomon's father asked him to come out into the barnyard.

There they stood under a large maple tree whose leaves had been scorched by the heat of the burning barn. Solomon wondered what his father wanted to talk to him about. He had never been treated in such a grown-up way before. Mr. Story said, "Son, your mother and I have been making plans for some time to move up to Vermont and settle some of the new land that has opened up. When the barn burned, we had to make up our minds. We have decided now is the time. I will have to go first to make a place ready for your mother and the little children. We have been wondering if you are old enough to go with me. It will be a long walk. There will be lots of hard work. We think you can do it. What do you think?"

Solomon was thirteen. He was large and strong for his age. He had heard about the settlers who were moving north. Some had gone from his home town of Salisbury, Connecticut. It seemed like a wonderful adventure to go off with his father into this new country. But when he tried to answer his father's question, his words tumbled out in a disordered manner, though the meaning was sure. "I would, I mean— Oh, yes, Father, I would like very much to go with you. But what about Mother and the children?"

Mr. Story put his hand on the boy's shoulder, looked him straight in the eye, then said, "Fine, my boy, you shall go. The rest of the family will come when we have a place ready for them. Now get ready for church, for I think the rest of the family is waiting."

All through the long sermon, Solomon was traveling north in his mind. He was seeing hills and mountains, rivers and forests, wild animals and Indians. Life in a small Connecticut town in 1774 was interesting, but it could not compare with the adventure of going north to Vermont and the Green Mountains.

For several days the activity around the Story home was intense. The early crops were gathered in. An old chicken house was made into a corncrib. The woodshed was filled to capacity. Vegetables were stored away in the dark cellar. Hay was piled high in a stack so that the cows could munch on it through the winter, and a carriage shed nearby was made into a temporary shelter for them. Mr. Story did everything he could to provide for his wife and children before he started off toward the north.

The first of September had come. With the summer work nearly done in Connecticut, they could start north and have crops planted and ready to harvest by the same time next summer in a new home.

Mr. Story chose to take a horse that was not worth much in trade. He would trade the horse for a canoe in Rutland. All the horse was needed for now was to carry their packs until they came to the waterway that would take them north.

Into the packs were folded blankets, warm clothes for winter, seeds for spring planting, corn meal for times when hunting might not be so good, salt, and tools for clearing land and building a log house. The number of necessities was small in those days.

When it was finally time to go, there was little ceremony. Some neighbors gave their good wishes for the journey. The younger children—Hannah, Susanna, Samuel, and Ephraim—watched the last-minute packing with excitement, and hugged and kissed their father and older brother when they were ready to depart.

Ann Story was not a woman of easy tears, but you could have seen two glistening spots in the corners of her eyes as she said her fare-well, hugged her son, and said to her husband, "Take good care of Solomon. Watch out for Zeke Jenny and the Indians. The Lord watch over you both."

Good stagecoach roads were few, but the trails leading from town to town were numerous. Men had been traveling back and forth among the New England villages for over a hundred years. The Story farm in Salisbury was in a pleasant valley in the highest hills in Connecticut. Salmon Creek ran through the lower end of the farm, and Solomon had always known what it was like to travel on trails, roads, and creeks.

On their first day of travel, they were fresh and eager. They connected with the stagecoach road to Canaan and headed north into Massachusetts. By evening, they were beyond the small settlement of Sheffield. Instead of staying at an inn, Amos and Solomon unpacked their horse and rolled up in their blankets under the stars. The September nights were clear and cool. Amos did not want to spend money unless it was absolutely necessary, so they planned to stay at taverns only when the weather was too bad and would harm their supplies. Amos and Solomon would dry off well enough if they got wet, but their precious supplies and tools had to be protected.

At Sheffield they picked up the trail that followed the Housatonic River. Here they were always sure of good fresh water to drink and brook trout ready to be flipped into their spider, as they called their frying pan with three long legs. The second night they were in the village of Stockbridge. A friendly farmer invited them to sleep in his hay barn, and during the evening he talked a long time about the new territory of Vermont. If he had been younger, he said, he would have set out for the new country. As he put it, "When you get to be my age your old body won't keep up with your young ideas."

Three days later, they crossed from Massachusetts into Vermont. Solomon was sure he had never seen such beautiful hills and valleys as lay before them when they ventured on into Vermont. Amos had told Solomon about his travels through these parts when he had served with the British Army during the French and Indian War, but no word picture could compare with the sights that kept unfolding before Solomon's eyes.

At one place south of a settlement called Pownal, Solomon ran ahead and climbed the highest tree he could find. Years later, when he looked back at those moments, he described them as different from any he had ever known.

All at once his boyish heart was overcome with the beauty of a new, untouched world that was his to explore and develop. He was young enough to have the thrill of it seep into the marrow of his bones, and yet old enough to know what it meant in work and risk. Already his feet bore the marks of the miles, and at night his muscles ached. The more difficult part of the journey lay ahead, yet he knew that this was his world and that he would never leave it.

Even as he felt the thrill of his new world, he had an uneasy feeling of fear and apprehension. What if Zeke Jenny were lying in wait to get the revenge he had threatened? Solomon looked at his father, and he seemed calm and unworried. Solomon said, as casually as he could, "I hope Zeke Jenny stays away from us."

Solomon's father looked at him curiously. "Are you worrying about that Tory still? Remember, Vermont is a big place, and there should be plenty of room for us all up here."

Solomon felt relieved but questioned his father more. "What makes a Tory? Are they always bad?"

"A Tory is anyone who is so loyal to the

King that nothing else matters. It is the way they believe. The King comes first. Some Tories are fine persons, quiet and friendly. Zeke Jenny was always a hotheaded bully. He has a mean streak in him that shows up no matter what he does. I couldn't be a Tory, because I put my home and family first. I believe in what is good for them." His father's answers seemed to satisfy Solomon, for soon the subject was changed.

Two days later, they came to Bennington, a busy village that stood at crossroads leading north, south, east, and west. The British had set up a military depot here, and valuable supplies were stored where they could be quickly moved in any direction by the large military wagons kept in readiness.

Here Amos and Solomon stayed a day and two nights in a tavern, to rest and get ready for the overland trek to Rutland. Traders were all about, and Amos enjoyed talking with them, though he bought nothing. He visited with other settlers who were moving north. They compared ideas and methods for clearing land. Also, they talked politics, for there had been a long-standing feud between New York and New Hampshire over the land called

Vermont. Those who traveled north from Connecticut and Massachusetts were claiming land under New Hampshire grants. New settlers were enlisted in the Green Mountain Boys—a local militia made up of settlers, hunters, and trappers who acted as rangers. There was much talk in Bennington about what the Green Mountain Boys had done to drive New York surveyors out of the territory. Amos had heard of this before, was in full sympathy with the movement, and joined with them. He went with Solomon to the Catamount House and made his intentions known. There was no signing of enlistment papers, but there was an exchange of words which were as binding.

For his part, Solomon talked seriously with other boys his age about cabin building, land clearing, and canoe making. All the arts of frontier life were discussed. Hunting was Solomon's favorite subject. He now had his own musket, and the way of loading it was important. The boys talked about how much powder to use with different kinds of shot, the best size shot for different kinds of game, and the kinds of game that could be caught without using valuable shot and powder. The woods were full of porcupines to be caught and clubbed. A porcupine was always good for one meal.

Solomon talked with two boys from Norfolk, Connecticut, about which would be worse to meet, a catamount or wolves. Solomon said, "You can always climb a tree and get away from wolves, but a big cat will come up a tree." The other boys agreed and added that the cat might get up the tree first and jump down on an unsuspecting traveler underneath. "That is why I keep my long knife sharp and always by my hand," Solomon said, as he patted the hunting knife under his belt.

The day's stopover in Bennington was restful and interesting. It also made Solomon aware of what lay ahead on the long trail. It was going to be adventure, but it was dangerous adventure—how dangerous, Solomon was to find out very soon.

3. ATTACKED BY WOLVES

Early in the morning, Amos and Solomon set out from Bennington on the long overland part of their journey. With steady traveling, they estimated that they could be in Rutland in four days. Their old horse had had a day's rest, and the heavy packs were strapped on securely.

Soon they were moving along the trail, out of sight of the last dwelling in the village. At one place they came to a height of land beyond Bennington where there was a natural clearing. Deer moss was heavy underfoot, and it was like walking on a thick carpet. From this spot they could look back and see the cluster of buildings that made up the village of Bennington. But soon this was behind them.

The trail led through timber that had never been cut. The trees were tall and straight. Some of them were so big around that Solomon and Amos together could not reach around them. Some were spruce and pine, and others were hardwoods—maple, oak, and basswood.

Father and son would walk for a long distance without talking. Then they would burst into conversation that would occupy them for hours. So it was when Solomon said, "Father, how will we know when we have arrived at our new home?"

Amos tried to explain: "We are entitled to one hundred acres in any one of the three townships John Everts has claimed. We look around until we find what we want, and then we stake it out."

"How much is a hundred acres?" asked Solomon.

"Well, a hundred acres can be figured in different ways," Amos answered. "It depends on the lay of the land. A hundred acres would be roughly a mile long and a thousand feet across."

"What kind of land do we want?" Solomon asked.

"There are several things we want on our land. We want a way to travel, so it would be good to be near a trail and a creek. We want a good water supply, so we will also look for a spring. We want level land, bottom land if possible, that will make up into good fields. Also, we want a good supply of trees, both softwoods and hardwoods. We want to be out where we can expand, and yet near enough to a town so we can get supplies, and also a place where someday we may have a school nearby." Amos talked slowly, as if he were picturing the land as he described it.

"How can you tell it is the land you want when it is all covered with trees?" Solomon asked.

"Oh, that's easy," Amos said. "The trees are part of the answer. When we get toward that country, we will be riding along in a canoe. When we see what looks like a good spot, we will pull to shore and examine it. We can walk over a hundred acres in an hour or two. If it doesn't have what we want, we will keep on going."

"Won't it be wonderful to have all the new land we want to choose from!"

Solomon had forgotten how far they had walked since they had started this talk. Now the shadows in the woods were long, and it would be dark in a short while. Amos suggested that they find a good place to camp for the night.

Before long they came to a rocky cliff which would serve as a shelter. From the wood ashes against the cliff, they knew it had been used before as a camping place. A brook ran nearby. In a short while they had cut enough wood to start a cheerful fire. Amos scooped up several small trout from the stream and began to fry them.

"Better cut some more wood," Amos said to Solomon.

Solomon wanted to know why.

"Never know when you may need it," his father answered. "Here in the woods, it is often necessary to keep a fire going all night."

"I don't see why," said Solomon. "We can't heat all outdoors, and our blankets are warm. We would just waste the wood, and I'm too tired to chop any more."

Amos said no more but took his ax and laid

up a good supply of firewood and piled it near the cliff. By the time he had finished, it was dark, and Solomon had already fallen into the deep sleep of a tired boy after a long day's hike.

Amos shortened the rope on the horse and moved its stake nearer the fire. He loaded his musket and Solomon's as well, and put them nearby. He fixed the fire so it would burn brightly and could be kept going with a large backlog and smaller logs that could be pushed into the fire every hour or so. Then Amos went to sleep also, but with one ear open, as they said along the frontier.

Amos had no way of knowing how long he had been asleep when he was awakened by a long howl. He had heard it before, and it made his skin creep, even though he was a brave man. The long howl was answered from deep in the forest. As he listened, he knew the meaning of the sounds. From several directions the howls were coming together, and he and Solomon were in the center of the circle. A wolf pack was gathering. Solomon slumbered peacefully, and Amos decided to let him sleep as long as possible.

There came a long period of silence. In the black of the lonely night, Amos wondered if he might have been imagining the sounds. He pushed the logs farther into the fire and threw on more wood. The shadows that jumped up and down in the edge of the clearing looked like living creatures, but he knew his eyes might be deceiving him.

It seemed like a long time since he had heard any howling in the woods. In spite of himself, he found that his head nodded in sleep. He too was tired from the long day's trek, and peering into the dark so intensely added to his weariness. But he was brought back to alertness when he heard a branch crack in the underbrush not a hundred feet from the fire.

Amos put more wood on the fire so that it blazed up brightly. Then he awoke Solomon, saying, "Son, there is a pack of wolves out there just a hundred feet or so. I don't know how long it will be until morning. We will probably have to make a fight of it. We will keep the fire burning brightly and be ready to shoot it out as best we can. Don't get excited. We will have to use our heads. These critters are wise. We'll have to be wiser."

Solomon was wide awake in no time. He thought about wood for the fire, and, when he saw the large pile of it against the cliff, he was glad his father had not listened to him the previous evening.

The wolves were moving about in a semicircle on the edge of the darkness. They were afraid of fire, but they grew bolder as they got hungrier. Amos and Solomon could now see the reflection of the fire in the eyes of the milling beasts.

"When they get real hungry they will eat each other," Amos said. "We will probably have to shoot some of them to keep them at bay. I am afraid our firewood won't last until morning. If it does, we are safe, for they seldom attack in daylight."

Solomon kept the fire burning brightly and the stone cliff acted as a reflector, sending the light out into the surrounding darkness. Solomon had moved to get another load of wood when the night shook with a deafening roar. Jumping, Solomon dropped his wood and ran to his father's side.

"I had to get that one," Amos said. "He started toward you, but he is dead in his tracks."

Amos reloaded his musket. The dead wolf lay on the edge of the circle of light. The other wolves were moving close by it. Solomon tried to count them, but they were moving in and out of the shadow so rapidly that he could not.

"There must be twenty or twenty-five," Solomon said to his father.

The firewood was beginning to get low. The pack horse, staked in close to the cliff, was restless. The circle of light was getting smaller and smaller, and morning was still a long way off. Amos shot again into the mass of shining eyes, and, from the howl that went up, he knew he had wounded a wolf. The snapping and growling that followed meant that the other wolves had turned on their wounded companion. The number of eyes in the darkness decreased for a while, and the noise of the feasting cannibals was eerie.

Soon the circle of light from the fire contracted even more, for the kindling that made the bright glow was all used. Now all they could do was push the large logs into the fire and shoot at the wolves as they crept closer.

The darkness enveloped the first wolf that was shot, and it was noisily devoured. While this was going on, Amos shot again, but he must have missed, for there was no howl from the pack. He quickly picked up Solomon's gun and told him to reload the other one. Now it became a contest of supplying the hungry wolves with food from their own pack until morning came.

Amos pulled the pack horse in close to the fire, as close as the horse would go, for a horse is almost as afraid of fire as of wolves. While Solomon reloaded the muskets, Amos fired into the pack. Sometimes he could tell he had wounded an animal from the sudden yelp that came; at other times there was only the noisy eating that went on among the wolves themselves. It seemed that morning would never come.

The cliff was against the eastern sky line. Finally, from the woods on the other side of the stream, they heard a bird sing. Then they saw streaks of light, and the first glow of morning showed in the east. Solomon was sure he had never felt so glad to see day come.

The forms milling about in the edge of the darkness retreated as the light of the new day advanced. Amos and Solomon never knew how many wolves there were in the pack that had attacked them during the night, but they counted the remains of seven wolves that had been devoured by their mates.

Solomon breathed with relief when they had loaded the horse and started on their way north. Never again would his father have to urge him to get a good supply of wood ready for the night. He did not care if some of it were wasted. Never was wood wasted in so good a cause.

4. A FRONTIER SETTLEMENT

The frightening experience of the night before faded with the light of the new day. Although it did not now seem possible that, lurking deep among the trees, there might be dozens of wild animals that would creep up under the cover of night to attack humans, Solomon had learned several things during the night that he would not forget. One was that the forest wilderness was alive, and that dangers existed for those who were not prepared to protect themselves. He had also learned that, even though his father said little, in order not to alarm the boy, he meant everything he said and always had a good reason for it.

Solomon asked his father how he knew so

43

much about wolves and how to fight them. Then Amos told about his experiences traveling in the north country during the French and Indian War. He said, "There are three things to beware of in the north woods. One is wolves, and I don't have to tell you about them after last night. But always, when you pick a campsite in the woods, think about protection from wolves.

"A second thing is big cats. They are harder to figure. You seldom ever see or hear one. They usually don't have much to do with people, but they will attack farm animals. They come in three sizes. The little ones are wildcats. They are mean when cornered but will stay away from humans otherwise. They weigh about fifteen or twenty pounds and look like a house cat with its tail cut short. Then there is a cat about twice as big. It has short, pointed ears and is a real fighter. Never shoot at one of these unless you have to, for they are mean when wounded. It is called a lynx. It will usually leave you alone if you do the same for it. It usually weighs about thirty pounds or so. The big fellow is the catamount. It is bigger than a large dog, is tan in color, and has a long tail. The other kinds have bobtails. This big fellow will kill deer and calves and has attacked people. It is really dangerous and usually stays in the hills and deep woods. It is hard to kill, and some I've heard about had to be shot several times before they stopped fighting.

"The third thing to watch out for is Indians. They don't like having whites come into their lands. They don't really come out and fight. They sneak in quietly and burn villages or isolated houses. They get mean when they have firewater—that's what they call rum. I don't know as I blame them much for feeling the way they do, but they can be dangerous for the settler."

This kind of a lesson made a deep impression after a night of danger. Solomon listened but had no questions then. He turned everything over in his mind many times, and for days afterward his questions showed it had been a lesson well learned.

The country was rugged and the trail was difficult, so progress was slow. Though game was plentiful, it took more time to prepare it than they had expected. The grouse usually surprised them so that they were not ready to shoot them. For two days they had to be satisfied with rabbit and trout.

On the third day, the horse began to limp. Amos felt it would be wisest to give the horse a rest, because he did not want to try to trade a limping horse for a canoe in Rutland. They pushed on slowly to a settlement called Sunderland, where they gave the horse a good rest for a day and a night. They camped near the log house of a settler from Connecticut, who was glad to hear about recent events in his old home state. He had been here for two years and had cleared several acres. He had a cow and enough corn to keep her. Solomon was given fresh milk, the first he had had since leaving home.

After a rest the horse felt better, and the limp was gone. The remainder of the trip to Rutland was slow but without special event. Instead of making the overland trip in four days, as they had expected, it took a week to cover the sixty miles of trail.

It was about noon of the seventh day when Amos said, "Look ahead. See those buildings? That's Rutland."

This was a real frontier town. Bennington

was more like a Connecticut town, with its streets and houses. Rutland had only two real houses, with a number of log cabins to be seen in all directions. A stockade, made of heavy logs driven into the ground, was the largest building. Here the settlers could go if there were a raid by Indians. A trading post and a tavern were the main buildings in the center of the settlement.

Many canoes were pulled up on the bank of a muddy stream. A few wagons cut deep ruts in the main street of the settlement. Horses were tied in front of the tavern, and men stood about in small groups, talking and laughing.

When Amos and Solomon led their horse toward the tavern, they were greeted in friendly fashion. A member of one of the groups said, "Aim to trade that horse for a canoe?" Running his thumb expertly around the horse's upper lip, he said, "Ain't much of a horse."

Amos had expected this, but he made no comment. He knew a horse was a valuable possession in these parts, even if it were not a prize animal. Instead of talking about trading, Amos asked, "How is the trail north?"

Immediately, the man changed his attitude.

He said, "The trail's bad. You'd do better to take the creek."

Amos said quietly, "I'll see," and went on toward the door of the tavern. The trader followed him and said, "I'll make you a good deal. A good canoe and trade even."

Amos paid little attention and said, "Maybe tomorrow. I want to look around."

Solomon watched his father sign up for a room, and, when they were alone, asked, "Why didn't you trade the horse? I thought that was what you wanted to do all along."

Amos explained: "I don't want to seem too anxious. If I act as though I might want to take the trail, I'll get the canoe and a couple of pounds of powder to boot."

Sure enough, that evening while they were eating big plates of venison stew, the trader came in again, looking for Amos. "I hear you are goin' to Salisbury. That's right on the creek. The trail there is rough, bad on a horse. You'll need a canoe anyway. I'll make you a good deal—a good canoe, some powder, and shot."

Amos looked at Solomon but didn't say anything at first. He went on eating for a while. Then the trader said, "What's the matter? Don't like my deal?"

Amos smiled politely and replied, "I think I'll look around a bit tomorrow before I make up my mind. I'll be right here if you want to talk some more."

After they ate, Amos and Solomon walked along the creek looking at canoes. Some had just come from the north. Some of the owners were looking for a good trade, for they needed a horse to go on south. Amos talked with several persons, in friendly fashion, about their experiences up north. The trader watched them from a distance.

Next morning he met them at breakfast. He said, "I have been thinking. I could use a good horse. I'll make you a real good deal. You pick a canoe. I'll add two pounds of powder, a pound of shot, and a good long saw for you and your boy to use." When nothing was said, he looked at Amos and then at Solomon and added: "Just for good measure I'll throw in a tub of bear grease and a big kettle for boiling sap."

Amos said, "That sounds fair enough. I'll look it over after breakfast."

The canoe Amos picked was made of birch bark with well-tarred joints. It was long and wide enough to carry all their supplies and yet light enough for a man and a boy to handle.

The trader watched. "You should be satisfied," he said. "It's the best one I have."

"It's a deal then," said Amos, and, with no more comment, they transferred their supplies from the tavern, took the powder, shot, saw, and other utensils from the trader, led the horse from the stable, patted it on the nose, and turned over the reins.

As they stepped into the canoe and started to shove off, the trader smiled and said, "How would you like to buy a couple of paddles cheap?"

Solomon looked quickly at his father and saw his face turn red down to his collar. Then he said quietly, "No, thanks."

With their hands they pushed out into the stream and let the current carry them along. "I thought I had figured on everything," said Amos, "but these traders are sharp. They have to be watched every minute."

They paddled by hand around the first bend in the creek. Then Amos pulled in toward the bank. He climbed ashore, looked for a tree just the right size, and, with his ax, felled it. In no time he had split it in two, trimmed it down, and, with his hunting knife, had fashioned two long and strong paddles.

"I never like to let a horse trader get the best of me," said Amos, as they paddled smoothly along Otter Creek.

"Did you see how angry he was when you didn't buy the paddles? He got red and sputtered. When the others laughed at him, he didn't like it either. He shook his fist at you," Solomon said.

"Yes, I saw that. He is one to look out for. If we come back this way, he will probably remember our deal and try to get even," Amos answered. "A horse trader doesn't like to be laughed at."

"What can he do to you?" Solomon asked anxiously.

"Not much, as I figure it. We'll be on the lookout for any tricks." Amos smiled as he dug his crude paddle deep into the clear water. "This is the homestretch," he added, "and it feels good."

5. A PLACE IN THE WILDERNESS

From Rutland to Salisbury was thirty miles as the crow would fly, but Otter Creek meandered through the valley like a long snake. It seldom followed a straight course for more than a few hundred yards.

After getting out of sight of Rutland, Amos and Solomon had many a good laugh at the clever horse trader and his trick of trading the canoe without paddles. Though the paddles they had fashioned left much to be desired, they kept the canoe on its course and helped the current enough to move them north several miles a day.

Toward evening of the first day out of

Rutland, they were gliding along quietly and smoothly when Solomon whispered to his father, "Look—ahead." There at the creek bank, drinking, was a beautiful buck with his antlers spread out over the water. Quickly Amos had his musket in hand and, taking aim, pulled the trigger. His accurate shot hit the deer just behind the shoulder, and he lurched headlong into the water.

"We feast for a couple of days," shouted Solomon, as they paddled toward the deer, which had even then ceased to struggle in the water. They pulled the canoe ashore and dragged the deer from the water. Amos showed Solomon how to proceed with dressing the meat. The hide was stripped, scraped, and rolled for curing when they had the time to work with it. The liver was removed for a nourishing liver stew that would be their supper. The haunches of venison were carefully cut and wrapped in birch bark for use the next day or two. The rest of the carcass that could not be used was left by the creek bank for other hungry creatures to find.

Amos and Solomon, with their supply of fresh meat, were soon on their way again. Amos said it was not a good idea to camp too close to the place where they had dressed the animal, for other forest animals would soon be hovering around.

Camping at night from the canoe was quite different from camping with a pack horse. Arrangements had to be made to secure the canoe and its contents. They could not go far from the water's edge, lest animals raid their food supply in the canoe. So they tried each night to camp at or near a clearing where a settler had already staked out his claim. In this way they had companionship and shared information.

The first night they stopped near Pittsford, a shallow place in the creek where a horse could wade across. Silas Pinney, from Litchfield, Connecticut, had a place here. He was more than hospitable, and Amos gave him a large piece of fresh venison in return for permission to camp near his cabin for the night. All the rest of the food Amos placed in the large kettle and pulled it up over a tree limb until it was safely out of reach of any prowlers.

Silas Pinney told about choosing his place. He had traveled farther north, but he did not like being far from other people and so had staked his claim near the ford, for he knew more people would be traveling that way. He knew about the three towns that John Everts had chartered. The northern town was called New Haven, after the big town in southern Connecticut. The southern town was called Salisbury, for most of the grantees came from Salisbury, Connecticut. He didn't know what to call the town in between, so, temporarily, he called it the Middlebury. Silas had looked at land in those towns, but it was too far north for him. "But it is some of the most beautiful land I ever saw," he added. "The creek is wide and deep up there, and the valley has rich bottom land that goes back miles from the creek in either direction."

This sounded like the kind of land Amos was looking for, so he asked, "How is the south boundary of John Everts grants marked?"

"Oh, that's easy," said Silas. "I was up that way when Everts was making the survey. You go about two days canoe trip from here. Then you come to a place where Otter Creek turns sharp west. At that spot another creek comes in from the east, so big you can't tell it from the Otter unless you notice which way the water's flowing. Right there where the creek turns west is the south boundary of John Everts' three towns. The north boundary is about where the creek goes into Lake Cham-Plain. And prettier country you'll never see anywhere." He paused a while, then added, "Sometimes I think I made a mistake in not staying there. The land is better than here. I guess I just didn't have the heart for being so far north. Now I can get to Rutland in a day.

Someday, maybe. But then I'll probably be too old."

The picture that Silas Pinney painted of the land to the north stirred Amos and Solomon so that they were off bright and early the next morning. By noon of the second day, they came to the place where a large tributary entered Otter Creek and the main stream turned sharply west. Here then, was the land they had traveled so far to see. And somewhere along these banks there was a hundred-acre plot just waiting for them to claim it.

How different they now felt! They were not hurrying to get somewhere far off. They were there. Here was their land for the taking. They glided along with the current, looking first on one side of the stream and then on the other. In this way they traveled for about two miles, before the creek made another sharp turn toward the north. The timber was heavy and came to the edge of the creek. In most places the creek bank was a sharp drop of four or five feet to water level. In the spring the water probably rose over the banks, but now, after a long summer, the water was well below the level of the land.

During the two miles they had traveled,

they had not found one place where they could draw the canoe ashore. Now they began looking for a place where they might spend the night. They had moved out well beyond the outposts of civilization as they had known it. Not a human being was within miles of them, they were quite sure.

Paddling along slowly and quietly, Amos peered ahead. He pointed to a small inlet on the east bank of the creek. "Let's pull in there and look around," he said.

This they did and set foot in Salisbury, Vermont, for the first time in their lives. Here they were to know joys and sorrows. Here they would add an important chapter to the life of the state.

Pulling the canoe in close to the overhanging bank, Amos made it secure. Together, they walked off into the woods to get the lay of the land. It was quite some distance before the land began to rise above the level of the creek. The trees were massive and straight and quite far apart.

"This is beautiful timber," said Amos. "If we had a sawmill it would be just right. But this is too big for us to use in a log house. We will need small trees about ten inches to a foot across. Let's spend the night here and then look farther on tomorrow."

The next morning they set out for further exploration. Two or three times they put ashore at likely looking spots, but each time they returned to their canoe. In some places the trees were too big, or not the right kind, or there was not enough variety; at other places the land did not rise enough from the creek bank to be sure of safety from spring freshets. Although they found many marshy spots, they did not find any really good springs.

Two or three miles upstream from the place where it turned sharply north, they noticed a bend in the creek with a small inlet that looked right for getting the canoe ashore. The land rose gently to the east, with a small plateau that could be seen through the trees. The trees were large and free from underbrush. Here they stopped for more exploration.

Amos went toward the low plateau. Here he stopped by a small patch of ferns and felt the ground. It was wet. He was sure there was a spring just below the surface. On the plateau the trees were more numerous and not so large. This probably meant that a table of rock was underneath. Although it could not grow such large trees, it would be a good place to build a house, because the frost would not go so deep, and frost damage to the house would not be so great.

Amos called to Solomon, who had been exploring north along the creek bank. "How do you think this would be for a cabin site?"

Solomon knew his father liked the spot, and he agreed. The creek was just out of sight, about two hundred yards away. The land was well above the level of spring floods. The trees were numerous and the right size. The low-lying land would be fertile for cultivation when cleared. "It looks like just the spot," Solomon said, "but is there a spring nearby?"

"How about that place where the ferns are?" his father suggested. Solomon ran to the spot and began to dig with his hands. He pulled away the ferns and some of the flat stones underneath. The hole that the rocks left began slowly to fill up with muddy water.

"Looks like plenty of water here, if we can find the exact place. We'll have to work on that later. For now, we can get all the water we need from the creek," Amos said.

"Is this the place, Father?" Solomon asked.

"I think it is, Son," Amos answered.

So, quietly and without ceremony, a homestead that was to become famous in the life of Vermont was chosen.

"Let's build a shelter here, and move our supplies up. Then we can really get to work," Amos said. And the first ax blade dug into the hardwood with a sound that rang through the forest in all directions.

Solomon didn't say anything to his father about it, but he thought to himself, "What if Zeke Jenny and some Indians should hear the sound of the ax and come to find out who is settling here?" But he put the thought out of his mind and went to work.

6. BUILDING A LOG HOUSE

"We might as well take time to build a good shelter," Amos said. "Then we can use it for a woodshed and tool house. We will put it near enough to the main house so it will serve our purpose now and later."

Solomon was given the task of carrying things from the canoe through the woods to the little high piece of ground where the house was to be. By evening, all the supplies were safely placed, and the canoe was hidden under some overhanging bushes in the inlet. The ax that Amos wielded fell fast and true, and, as the trees toppled, Solomon trimmed off the small branches.

They worked until they could not see any

63

longer because of darkness. Then the camp-fire brought its glow to the woods, and two tired settlers stretched out before it. The late September night was frosty, and the chill cut deep into muscle and bone. This was all the incentive needed for finishing the woodshed as quickly as possible.

Breakfast next morning was strips of fried venison, corn-meal mush fried in the animal fat, and hot water to drink. Amos said, "It tastes so good because we are cold and hungry."

During the day they cut logs—some twelve feet long and some ten feet long. They found four large flat stones and moved them to the places where the corners of the woodshed would be. A smaller stone was placed where the doorpost would be. Amos had brought only four sets of hinges, for they were heavy to carry, but this woodshed would have a door. This would be their home while they built the log house, for they had to be warm, or as warm as possible.

First Amos notched the logs so that they would fit securely into each other when placed at right angles. He took a ten-foot piece that was straight and solid and split it down the

middle. The flat sides they placed on the flat
rocks, and then, piece by piece, they built up
the walls until they were above their heads.
On the side where the door was to be placed,
Amos added two more logs. This would give
the roof the pitch needed to let the rain run
off.

Then strong poles, notched to fit the front
and back of the shed, were placed from the
low side to the high side of the walls. While

Amos split some large logs into wide planks, he asked Solomon to cut squares of earth with deermoss on it. These were to be banked against the logs that fitted next to the earth so that no wind could blow through. Amos pointed out one place, and said, "don't put any moss there. We will need that to take care of the smoke."

Solomon was puzzled. How could a hole next to the ground take care of the smoke? So he asked his father, "How will that work?"

"That is a little trick I learned when we camped during the war. Leave a small hole on one side near the ground, and another one near the top on the other side, and the draft will take out most of the smoke. The other hole will be up here," and he pointed to a spot just under the roof where he was laying up the split boards.

"Aren't we having a chimney?" asked Solomon.

"No, not in the woodshed. We'll have one in the house when we get to it, but here we just need a small fireplace to cook on and keep the chill off," Amos replied.

"But look at all the holes between the logs," Solomon said with alarm.

"You'll take care of those," Amos said. "Do you remember that spot in the bank about a quarter of a mile below the inlet, where the cliff was steep and the soil was gray? That was clay, and we can use it for chinking the cracks. We'll go back there and fill the tub and the kettles. That will be just right for the holes between the logs."

After they finished placing the rest of the wide boards on the roof, they cut some notched boards to hold them secure. "That will keep out anything but a driving west wind," said Amos. "When that comes, we will just get wet."

Then Solomon gathered up the tub and kettles, and they started downstream in the canoe to get clay. The clay was moist and sticky, and Amos explained that when it dried it was quite hard. If it baked in the sun it would become almost as hard as a brick. The first load they took back filled most of the cracks, and made their woodshed quite secure against wind and rain.

"Now we will have to make a place for the fire," said Amos. He and Solomon looked for large flat stones. These they placed against the wall away from the door. "We will not be able to build a big fire here, but it will be better than no fireplace at all," Amos added.

Three days after landing, they had a shelter from the weather, a safe place for their supplies, and a base of operations for their next and more important task, the building of the log house.

Along one wall of their little shed, Solomon had laid up a pile of hemlock boughs. These made a soft bed for their blankets to rest on. Solomon was so tired at night that he thought nothing could waken him. But that night he jumped in his sleep and sat up straight. He had heard a sound from the woods that frightened him. When his eyes became adjusted to the darkness, he saw that his father was also awake, standing near the door with his musket in his hand.

Whispering, Solomon said, "What is it, father?"

"I wondered if you would hear it," said Amos. "This is a sound you will have to get to know, and never let it fool you. I am never quite sure myself, but in this spot I think we can be fairly sure that it is a wildcat of some kind."

They listened quietly for a while, and then

it came again—a long, pitiful wail, piercing the forest silence. It sounded like a woman being tortured and crying out in unbearable pain. The cry echoed through the forest and then was followed by a silence that seemed even more foreboding. When would the next wail come? And from what direction?

Amos said that he had heard such cries before. He knew of men who had set out in the darkness seeking a woman in distress, only to be attacked by a big cat. It was a strange, eerie cry. It was almost impossible to tell how far away the source was or from what direction it had come. It lay heavily on the night air in all directions.

"Never go off alone to trace a cry like that," said Amos, as they tried to settle down again for the night. But the wailing continued from far in the woods until daylight came. Even as they talked about it the next morning, the memory of the cry made Solomon shiver.

"Sometimes Indians have been known to give such a cry to lead their enemies into ambush. Always be careful when you hear it. And always remember that a cat can see at night and you can't," Amos cautioned his son.

For several days the forest rang with the sounds of the axes that Amos and Solomon swung. Amos cut the trees, and Solomon trimmed off the branches. Day by day, they widened the circle around their woodshed. The large logs they rolled to the spot of ground they had chosen for their log house. The larger branches they cut and piled for firewood. The small branches they piled around the stumps and burned.

One day, as they worked, they were surprised to hear a call from the woods toward the creek. A middle-aged man and two strong young men were walking toward them. They smiled in friendly fashion. The middle-aged man held out his hand and said, "You must be Amos Story. I heard you were coming. My name is Smauley, Benjamin Smauley, and these are my sons, Dan and Eli. We are going to Rutland for some trading. Can we get you anything?"

Amos had heard of Smauley, one of the grantees. He was glad to get to know him. They sat down on some stumps and talked for a while. They shared information and experiences, and then had a light lunch. Before they left, Mr. Smauley said, "When you are ready to hoist the rafters, let us know, and we will give you a hand. We're just about seven miles up the trail from here, Middlebury."

Amos seemed surprised. "What trail?" he asked.

"Oh, didn't you know about the trail? It goes right by here. It may even be on your property. I judge it's about a thousand yards east of here. Yes, it's an Indian hunting trail. Comes down from the lake and crosses near our farm. You can't miss our place. If you take the creek you can see it, and if you take the trail you turn west at the second large stream you come to, and that leads through our farm. When you need us, send the boy up, and we'll give you a day, all hands." Mr. Smauley shook hands again and started off to the creek.

"Looks as though we have nice neighbors," Amos said, as he watched the three visitors make their way through the woods. "In about two weeks we could use some extra hands getting the rafters into place. But we have lots to do before then. We'd better get busy." So Amos picked up his ax and was soon at work again.

Solomon felt good to know that there were neighbors nearby to call on for help if it were needed.

Day by day more trees fell and more logs were trimmed. They were notched and rolled into place. It took all the strength of a man and a boy to lift the logs into place in the walls of the house.

"You see how it works," said Amos. "It is just like building the woodshed, except larger."

The house was sixteen by twenty-four feet, with two rooms downstairs, and upstairs a loft which would be reached by climbing a ladder. Here would be sleeping space for the children.

"It begins to look like a house," said Solomon one evening, as he stood off looking at what they had done during the day.

"Yes," Amos said, "when we get the rafters up and the roof on, it will look like a real house."

7. RAISING THE ROOF

"We'll have to have everything ready to put together when the Smauleys come," Amos said one day. "We'll need thirty rafters all notched and ready to fit together. Nothing goes worse at a house-raising than to find that the timbers won't fit. Then it all has to be done over again while everyone stands around wasting time."

"What will we use for the roof? We don't have any shingles," Solomon said.

Then Amos explained how the roof would be put on. First they would have to allow for two long pieces on the top of the side walls. These would stick out two or three feet and would have deep notches to take a long cross

73

timber on which the roof boards would be finally placed. The rafters would be hoisted up into place and notched at one end to fit into the wall logs, and at the other end to fit into the rafter that came from the other side wall. Each rafter was smoothed on one side with a strange-looking kind of ax called an adze. It was specially made for trimming off the face of a log.

The thirty trees that were trimmed for rafters were spruce, light and strong and easy to work with. When these were put into place two feet apart, smaller crosspieces were fitted into shallow notches twelve or fifteen inches apart. On these crosspieces the roof boards would fit when they were laid across them.

Solomon was still puzzled by this explanation, so Amos tried to show in another way how it worked. "It's like this," he said. "The rafters hold up the roof. They have the strength. The crosspieces hold the rafters apart and also give a smooth surface for the roof boards to lie on, and the roof boards shed the rain or snow. See how it works?"

Solomon was still puzzled. "But what keeps the rain from coming in between the boards?"

So Amos started to explain some more. "Do

you see those wide boards I have so carefully cut out of the center of the logs? The ones I have laid out in the sun to dry? Do you notice what has happened to them?"

"Yes," said Solomon. "They have all curled up, with a valley in the center."

"That is right," Amos went on. "If we had well-seasoned wood, we would not have to do that, but it works out all right for us. When I lay the green board in the sun, it dries fast on one side. That makes the top side shrink, and the board gets a shallow valley on one side. When the roof boards are laid, the first layer goes on with the valleys facing up. Then over the joint where the boards meet we place a board with the valley down. See how it works? The valleys drain the rain from the little hill in between, and it all runs down to the ground."

Solomon was impressed by this clever way of putting the roof together. He hurried on with his questions. Always his father would answer him patiently, for he knew this was important education for his son, and in this venture they were partners.

It took a week to trim and shape the rafters. Even then, there were not enough roof boards to cover the roof. They set a date for inviting the Smauleys to come for the roof raising. Solomon remembered the date well, for it was his father's thirty-sixth birthday. Yes, it was the seventeenth of October, just about a month after their arrival in Salisbury.

Solomon had thought many times about what Mr. Smauley had said when he left a couple of weeks before. "When you need us, send the boy up, and we'll give you a day, all hands." Solomon was a brave lad, and he was willing to make the trip alone if his father wanted him to do so, but, a number of times, he had thought of the trail and what it would be like to travel seven miles through the woods. He wondered what he would do if he met Indians. Would he see them first or would they see him? Should he run or hide? These questions bothered him more than he would admit.

It was quite a relief, therefore, when his father said, "Tomorrow we will go up to the Smauleys and invite them to come down next week for my birthday party."

Solomon was pleased to know his father was going too, but he did not want to appear too pleased, or his father might think he was afraid or unwilling to go alone. So he said, "Why do you want to go along, Father?"

"For several days I have wanted to go and look at that Indian trail. I hope it doesn't pass too close to us. I might not have chosen this place if I had known it was there. Now I want to get a good look at it and find out where it runs. Also," said Amos, "I want to see what kind of a place the Smauleys have. And a day away from the ax and saw will be good for us both. We've been working steadily and hard. We need a little change. Maybe we'll do a little hunting, too."

The next morning they started east through the forest, and, about a mile away from their clearing, they came upon a well-worn path through the woods. It was narrow and obviously only a footpath, but it could be clearly seen winding its way through the woods in both directions. Amos started south, and Solomon wondered if his father were confused about the direction to Middlebury.

"I want to see which way it goes below our place," explained his father. They followed the path for a mile or two and found that it met the creek at the point where it made the sharp turn west. So, having satisfied their

curiosity that much, they turned around and
started north. They talked about trees and
birds and animals as they walked. They kept
a lookout for game, for food was always important. Amos had large shot in his musket,
and Solomon's was loaded with smaller shot.
Amos was ready for a deer if he saw one, and
Solomon would be ready for quail or wild
turkey.

They crossed the first creek that Mr.
Smauley had mentioned, and then headed for
the next one. Before they reached it, it began
to rain, and they covered the ends of their
muskets to keep the moisture out, for wet
powder doesn't fire. When they came to the
second stream, the trail went across, but they
turned sharply west along the bank and, before long, came upon the clearing they took to
be the Smauleys'. Smoke rose from a sprawl-
ing stone chimney. They heard noise from the
barn but at first saw no one. Amos called,
"Halloo the house."

A woman came to the door and smiled in
a friendly manner. "Come on in," she greeted
them. "You are soaking wet. Let me get you
something hot to drink. Benjamin and the

boys are not far off. I know you must be the Storys. I heard about you."

Solomon always thought about his mother many times during the day, and sometimes dreamed about her at night. But he was startled now to hear how a woman's voice sounded. It had been weeks since he had seen a woman, and strange feelings of loneliness came over him.

Mrs. Smauley went to the door and blew a long blast on a ram's horn, and in no time at all Mr. Smauley and the boys appeared. Greetings were exchanged, and a noon meal was served. Solomon thought to himself that women had a way with food that men didn't have. The invitation for the roof-raising birthday party was given and accepted, and then the Storys were on their way home through the woods.

That night the rain turned to snow, and Amos said that they were not getting the roof on their house any too soon. But the next day was clear and warm, and the snow did not last, even though it was a sign of things to come.

There were just a few days left now before

the roof timbers would be lifted into place. They worked carefully, measuring every timber and then fitting them together, as they lay on the ground, to make sure the notches came at the right places. Solomon was set to cutting hickory pegs to hold the rafters together, while Amos used the auger to drill the holes.

October seventeenth was clear and mild, a typical Indian-summer day. The sun had not been up long before the friendly call of the Smauleys came up the path from the creek. All four had come. Benjamin carried tools and Mrs. Smauley had a ginger cake made with corn meal. As a present, Benjamin handed Amos some nails, and said, "I thought maybe you could use a few. They come in handy sometimes."

Amos thanked him and said that he had brought along a few but hadn't had to use any yet.

They wasted no time. Soon, strong and skilled arms went to work to lift the rafters into place and peg them securely together.

"You've done a good job notching these," complimented Mr. Smauley. "It makes a big difference when things fit right."

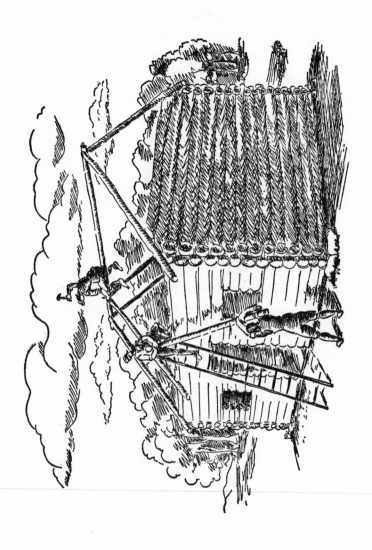

One of the Smauley boys sat astride the rear wall and one astride the front wall. Amos and Benjamin pinned the tops of the rafters together and lifted them up over the ends of the walls, and together they moved them toward the center of the cabin. The first rafters were braced into place at the center, and then others were placed two feet to each side until all were in place. The crosspieces were then fitted, and the rafters made solid and secure.

At noon they stopped for a big venison stew Mrs. Smauley had made. When the last rafters were in place, a recess was declared and the birthday cake was served. As they sat down on planks in the dooryard, Mrs. Smauley started to sing, "Praise God from Whom All Blessings Flow," and all the rest joined in. Mrs. Smauley started singing so high that the men's voices could not keep with her on the high notes, but to Solomon it sounded good, and he swallowed a lump in his throat as he thought of the times he had heard that hymn sung at home and at his church.

When the cake was eaten, Benjamin said, "Now let's get on as many roof boards as possible. We'll have to go in an hour." Before the hour was over, most of the boards had been laid in place, and the cabin had a finished look, though there was much more work to do before it was really livable.

Thanks were expressed as the Smauleys started toward their canoe.

When they were gone, Amos and Solomon stood for a long time looking at what had been done during the day.

"That was a real fine birthday present, wasn't it?" said Solomon.

Amos nodded his head, stood quiet for a long while surveying the new cabin, and then said, "I hope your mother will be happy in it."

8. FACING THE NORTHERN WINTER

The mild Indian-summer days served well for closing in the cabin. The roof boards were made secure by split logs that were placed across them and pegged into place with hickory pins. The only nails that Amos used were at the peak of the roof where two small, well-trimmed boards were nailed tightly together. However, he did use some heavy bolts to hang the door and the shutters for the windows.

Because there was no glass for windows, Amos had stretched raw, uncured deerskin across the frame and rubbed it with grease. This let light in, but it was not possible to see through it. In the daytime the cabin was dimly lit, and at night the only light came from the fire in the fireplace.

Amos and Solomon were still living in their woodshed. This they would do for a while, because it was easier to heat the small building while they were working on the fireplace and chimney in the log house.

When the cabin was roofed over and the walls were made tight with a mixture of clay and wood chips, Amos went to work to finish the fireplace and chimney. Solomon brought load after load of clay from the bank of the creek, and Amos used it to bind together the flat stones that he had built into a large fireplace. The back of the fireplace sloped outward toward the room to reflect the heat. A large iron hook, brought specially for the purpose, was built into the side of the chimney so that a kettle could be swung in over the fire or out into the room.

Amos explained that the heat of the fire would bake the clay until it was almost as hard as the stone around it. As the fire roared in the newly finished fireplace, Amos outlined to Solomon the important work they had yet to do before the house was ready for

a family to live in. "We have to make furniture," he said, "but that we can do when
the winter storms set in. We have to do some
real hunting and get a bear or two before
they hibernate. We must also make a trip to
the nearest trading post and get salt, corn
meal, and other foodstuffs to last through a
long winter. Then, when the days are good
for working outside, we can use all the time
possible to fell trees and prepare the fields
for planting next spring."

"Why do we need to get bears?" asked
Solomon.

"Just before the bear hibernates, he eats
lots of food and stores away many layers of
fat. This fat can be used for many things. We
can use it to grease pots and to make soap, and
it even makes a good substitute for butter,"
replied Amos, as Solomon shuddered a little
at the thought of using bear grease for butter.

"How do you make soap from bear grease?"
asked Solomon.

"Wait until we get the bear, and then I will
show you." And Amos continued with his
plans for the months that lay ahead. "We had
better take the trail down to Rutland. We can
travel light, with only our muskets, going

down, and carry our packs of supplies on the way back. The canoe would hold more, but we can handle all we will need on our backs, and I'd like to see what the trail is like."

"Can we stay with settlers on the way?" wondered Solomon, as he remembered the night when the hungry wolves attacked them, and the other night when the wildcat wailed.

"Yes," Amos answered. "I am sure we can arrange that. Everyone is hospitable along the trail. We would always do the same for anyone else."

The next day Solomon went off into the woods to gather butternuts from a tree Amos had located. His father stayed back at the clearing to cut some small boards to fit tightly under the eaves. There were many such small tasks yet to be done. Though they did not look like much when they were finished, they took time and patience. However, every little effort to make the house tight from the wind would be a blessing when the zero cold came.

Solomon had picked up all of the nuts he could find on the ground. He even tried shaking the tree and throwing sticks up into the branches to knock off more of the nuts. He did not want to go home with his bag only half filled, so he ventured farther on into the woods. He thought he heard a strange noise, and went on cautiously to investigate.

From well up in a tree he heard a growling noise. He tried to look up into the tree, but it was an oak, and its dried brown leaves were still so thick that he could see nothing more than a large black form that seemed to be making the noise. He turned at once and ran as fast as he could to tell his father what he had seen.

"Sounds like a bear in a bee tree," said Amos, as he took down his musket.

Off they went into the woods, and among the thousands of trees Solomon led his father directly to the foot of the tree where he had dropped his bag of butternuts when he ran back to the clearing.

"Sure enough," Amos said. Taking careful aim, he pulled the trigger. At first nothing happened. All was quiet up in the tree. Amos began to reload his musket at once. And then there was the sound of falling, and they could hear the heavy body of the bear as it hit branch after branch and then landed not far from their feet. He was quite dead, though his massive body still heaved and jerked.

Amos stood back cautiously. "It is a good shot that kills a bear the first time. I must have hit him just right. We can be thankful we shot him so near home. I feared we might have to drag one for miles. Run back to the cabin and get an ax and a piece of rope."

When Solomon returned with the ax and rope, the bear was quiet. His father showed Solomon how to select and cut boughs and lash the bear to them. They started to drag the bear through the woods. "Don't forget your butternuts," said Amos, and Solomon ran back to get them and threw the bag on the boughs with the bear. Together, they dragged the heavy body off through the woods to the cabin, where they would prepare it for winter use.

First they removed the large black bear-skin that would make a good rug for the cabin floor. Then they boiled out many pounds of bear fat. The bear steaks also were carefully cut, salted, and hung to cure. "One more bear that size, and we will be set for the winter," thought Amos.

It was the second week in November when Amos and Solomon started south on their trading trip. They had been so busy building that they had not tried to get furs to take for trading. They traveled light and fast, for they did not want to be caught on the trail by an early storm. Mr. Smauley had given them the names of neighbors to the south, and they had figured that, with good traveling, they could be in Rutland on the third day.

It was not yet noon on the third day when they walked into the trading post at Rutland. They were giving their order for hardware, salt, and other supplies, when they were interrupted by loud talking. At first they paid no attention, and then it came closer to them. Amos turned and recognized the trader who had gotten his horse in return for the canoe without paddles. He was babbling incoherent insults and shaking his fist at Amos. Amos did not answer. The manager of the trading post took the man by the arm and led him to the door. "We want no trouble in here. Get out!" he ordered.

When he came back to his customers, Amos asked, "What is the matter with him?"

The manager explained: "That man drinks too much. He is always trying to play jokes on others, but he can't stand anyone who turns the tables on him. He tried to make game of you when he traded you a canoe without paddles, but you didn't fall for his game. He had lots of watchers on hand to see the fun, and, when you went quietly on your way, he was made the brunt of the laughter. They haven't stopped tormenting him yet. He is angry at you. He has threatened to horsewhip you when you came to town. But I don't think he will cause you any real trouble. He is a bully."

Solomon was concerned about his father. He didn't want to see him horsewhipped. "What are you going to do, Father?" he asked.

"Nothing," Amos answered, "unless I have to. Then I may have to teach Mr. Trader some manners."

When they left the trading post an hour or so later, they thought the trader might have cooled off, but it appeared that he had added fuel to the fire in him and was more drunk and noisy than before. They started toward the tavern where they planned to eat and spend the night. Halfway there stood the trader, leering at them and shouting insults.

A crowd had gathered nearby to share in any excitement that might develop.

"If you come any closer I'll give you the whipping of your life. How dare you make sport of an honest trader?" he cried. He swung back his arm with a long bull whip in his hand.

Deliberately, Amos set down his pack and said to Solomon, "You stand here by the packs."

While he walked slowly forward but was yet well out of range of the whip, the trader cut the air with it, and its snap made a report like a rifle shot.

Amos kept moving slowly forward. He watched the whip, but he also watched the eyes of the trader. He thought he was probably drunk enough to have lost his judgment of distance. Again, when Amos was just out of range of the long whip, the trader lashed out with it. As soon as the loud report came from just a foot or so before his face, Amos sprang forward. Before the trader could get another chance to draw back his whip, Amos had him by the wrist. With a quick twist and a sharp jerk, he had the whip in his own hands.

Amos stepped back a few paces. The trader was surprised and baffled. He did not want to run. He did not want to feel the smart of his own whip. He became suddenly silent and uttered no more threats or insults.

Then, without saying a word, Amos drew back his arm and gently but firmly snapped the whip so that it encircled the ankles of the bully. With a quick motion of his arm, he pulled the feet out from under the bully and sat him in a puddle of water at the edge of the roadway. Then, throwing the amazed trader the other end of the whip, he said firmly, "Try acting like a gentleman after this."

The crowd roared with laughter at the trader as he tried to get out of the puddle. His feet were still hobbled by the end of the whip, and for a while all he could do was wallow in his uncomfortable spot. All the bluster and strong language had gone out of him.

Amos walked back to Solomon, picked up his pack, and walked on down the street to the tavern.

"That was good, Father," Solomon exclaimed.

"Never pick a fight, Son, but neither

should you let any one take your rights away," said Amos.

Early the next morning they were on their way back toward their clearing, prepared for the winter. The forest was full of food and fuel. The well-built cabin was tight against the winter storms. Amos was sure that they would be able to get a wild turkey for a feast of Thanksgiving when they moved from the woodshed into their new home.

"How do you make soap out of bear fat?" asked Solomon, when he came through the door and saw the bearskin on the floor.

"In a day or so, I'll show you," Amos said, as he took off his pack, stretched his arms, and said, "Let's have some corn-meal mush and go to bed."

As he busied himself with the frying pan, he looked at Solomon and said as casually as he could, "We had better keep our eyes sharp. You will be interested to know that our old neighbor, Zeke Jenny, is in these parts." "I asked at the trading post if they knew him, and they said they had seen him but didn't know where he had settled. They thought perhaps he was hunting and trapping farther up the creek."

A chill of apprehension ran up Solomon's spine, but he said nothing. It was unpleasant to think that, even then, an enemy might be lurking in the woods.

9. WINTER DAYS

The winter days were short. Amos and Solomon ate their breakfast in the cabin lighted only by the glow from the fireplace. Then they worked outside while there was light and had their evening meal again by firelight.

During late November and early December the days were crisp and cold. On a good day, as many as twenty trees would fall to earth. The trees in the deep forest were long and straight, for they worked hard to get their leaves up to the sun.

The woodshed was well filled with wood, cut and split for the winter, so the extra trees that fell were stacked on the spot in four-foot lengths. Next year, when they were seasoned, they would split more easily. The small branches were burned near where they had been trimmed, for Amos said the wood ashes were good preparation for planting the soil.

One day Amos said, "Son, clean the ashes out of the fireplace, but don't throw any of them away. I'll need them to make soap."

Solomon did as he was told but wondered how the wood ashes would mix with the bear grease to make soap. When he carried the ashes out the door, his father told him to put them in a large birch-bark funnel he had made. Then he poured water in over the ashes and waited for it to seep through into a kettle he placed beneath the funnel. All this was done in the warm sun in the middle of the day, so that the water would not freeze. Slowly the water seeped through, drop by drop. Amos explained that the water leached out the salts in the wood ashes. When these salts mix with grease they cause a chemical reaction and soap is the result of the chemical process. The process had been used for a long, long time.

That evening they had a frying pan full of soap. They cut it into pieces and stored it

for use. Not much was used on frosty morn-
ings, but even Solomon valued a cake of soap
now and then.

One morning at breakfast of fried venison
and corn meal with gravy, Amos asked, "How
would you like to have some honey?"

Day after day they had much the same food,
and, although it satisfied their hunger, it did
get tiresome, and the thought of honey was
most pleasant. "But how will we get it?"
Solomon asked.

"I have thought about that tree the bear
climbed. There was honey on his claws. He
had surely found some honey just as you
found him. The bees are all quiet now for
the winter. If we cut the tree down we can
get the honey. Let's do that today."

Amos did not need to urge Solomon. This
seemed more like a picnic than anything that
had happened since the trip to Rutland.

They had no trouble finding the tree again.
It was a large oak that had evidently been
struck by lightning. The scar high up on its
trunk was the place where the bees had stored
their honey. Amos and Solomon had learned
how to chop together, one swinging from one
side and one from the other of a tree. This

was a big tree, but an hour's work brought it to the ground. They trimmed enough branches to bring the large scarred surface into reach. Then they had to do some cutting to expose the honey. "Isn't that beautiful," said Amos, as he pointed out the symmetrically built honeycomb filled with honey. With their hunting knives, they cut the comb away from the wood and put it into their big sap kettle. Solomon licked the blade of his knife and smacked his lips. They put a long pole through the handle of the kettle and, together, carried off their prize of the day. Amos thought there was at least forty pounds of honey in the kettle, enough to last them until the maple sap began to run. The cornmeal mush tasted far better when it was dripping with honey.

The days settled into a routine. An hour or two morning and evening were needed for hunting. Before the turn of the year they had explored the land in all directions on their numerous hunting trips. Aside from the Indian trail, there was no sign of human existence. No person was seen for weeks at a time. Travel on the creek was dangerous because of pieces of floating ice.

The rest of the time was given over to extending the clearing. It was a slow and arduous task, using much energy and strength. Some days all of their efforts produced only a few feet more of opened land. As branches dried they were burned. This made big brown patches in the snow for a while, until more snow fell and covered the scar.

At Christmas Amos and Solomon thought and talked much about the rest of the family back in Connecticut. They wondered how they were doing and what a Christmas would be like there without them. They pictured other years with the good food and the church services. On Christmas eve Amos took out the little leather-covered Bible Ann had packed with his things and read aloud by firelight the story of the first Christmas. Then on Christmas day they made a pan of johnnycake and covered it with honey. It tasted good. "Next Christmas we'll all be here together," said Amos.

Shortly after the first of the year 1775, a northwest wind began to blow. It brought heavy snows that fell for three days. The woodshed was just thirty feet away, but it seemed like a long journey through the driving snow and the deep drifts. But they had enough rabbit and venison and wild turkey to eat, and enough firewood to keep them warm if they stayed close enough to the fireplace.

"This is good weather for making furniture," said Amos. He had stored some choice boards on crosspieces under the rafters for furniture making. Now he selected some pieces, and, using a drawknife with skill, he smoothed them off for a table top. Working slowly and with the patient skill of a craftsman, he showed Solomon how to join the boards. His uncle Jacob was a cabinetmaker in Salisbury, Connecticut, and in his shop Amos had learned many of the skills of a good woodworker.

The legs of the table were turned from oak branches and fitted into auger holes Amos drilled into the crosspieces under the table top. The table was strong, heavy, and could be used for doing the kitchen work as well as for family eating. It was not a finished piece of furniture, but it was a serviceable table that would last for years.

Benches were fashioned in like manner. A large open cupboard was made for a kitchen wall. A low bed was made for one corner of the second room, along with a large blanket chest. Pegboards for the walls were made for hanging clothes in an open closet. "Three or four more good storms, and we will have our new home furnished," Amos said with a laugh.

Solomon had noticed his father looking at the lower branches of the big maple trees near the edge of the clearing. Every few days he would reach up and feel of them to see if they were moist at the place where he had bent the twig. One day he called to Solomon, "Look, the sap's running." It was in February. The February thaw had set in. The dripping of melted snow from the roof was a pleasant sound as the warmth of the sun beat down on the south side of the roof of the cabin.

Amos used his auger to drill out the center of some small pegs. These he drove into another hole he had drilled into the trunk of the maple tree. Then, with his hunting knife, he made long cuts in the bark leading down to the peg. On the peg he hung one of his kettles. Soon he had drilled and pegged as many trees as he had kettles. The big sap kettle was cleaned of the remaining honey, and, before long, sap was beginning to boil. The sap ran well, and the kettle boiled day and night. It filled the cabin with a thick and heavy odor.

One of their problems was that they had so few containers. So Amos let the sap boil until it tested for sugar. This meant that, when hot sap was poured over snow, it would immediately turn to sugar. They turned nearly all of the sap to sugar rather than sirup because they had no place to store the sirup. Of course, they used some sirup on their corn-meal mush, but the sugar was the main item they produced from the sap.

By the middle of March, when the good sap run was over, they had carefully stored away in birch-bark containers over a hundred pounds of maple sugar, as Amos figured it. Solomon had cracked most of his butternuts while he watched his father make furniture, and he found that, by putting a handful of nutmeats in a cake of maple sugar as it hardened, he made himself really good candy.

The days were getting longer now. The worst of the winter was over. The house was built and furnished. The clearing had been slowly pushed out from the cabin until a good two acres were ready for planting. A shallow well had been dug at the point of the spring, and it had a steady supply of good water. But best of all, Solomon had learned many of the arts of a settler.

Amos explained to Solomon that the crops would have to be planted around the stumps for a few years until the stumps rotted away. He said, "We will plant Indian fashion. They hoe up little hills of earth and plant the corn. It is not like the even rows on the farm back in Connecticut, but is should work as well. Then around the stumps we plant cucumbers, melons, squash, and pumpkins. These keep well into the winter, and they don't need much care. The corn needs to be hoed and the beans have to be tended. The Indians taught us much about how to grow vegetables in the wilderness."

Amos had brought two hoes without handles. They were easier to carry that way. Now he made handles for both of them, and together, father and son, they began the processes of spring planting. The last traces of the snow could still be seen on the distant hills and in the edges of the forest, but the warm sun in the middle of the day and the early sunrise and late sunset told them better than anything else that spring had come.

And they were happy. Winter in the north country was long and hard. So the spring was all the more welcome when it came to relieve the ordeal of the long, cold months.

10. TRAGEDY STRIKES

It was well along in May. The days were beautiful and mild. The nights were crisp and cool. It was perfect weather for working and sleeping.

Most of the planting had been done. The snakelike rows of corn wound in and out around the stumps. The pumpkin vines had begun to crawl up the stumps.

One day at noon Amos said, "That big maple has to come down. It is shading the south end of the cornfield and will keep the corn from growing. We might as well do it now. Get the axes."

Together, they started—as they had so many other times before—the regular, rhythmic swing of their axes against the hardwood. They cut in deep on the forest side so that the tree would fall away from the clearing and into the woods. With the skill of much practice, they cut the yawning scar on the south side of the tree. The heavy old monster began to creak. Amos cried out, "Look out, it's falling."

And then it happened. Solomon had jumped back into the clearing as he had done hundreds of times before when the warning call had come. But, as his father started to jump back, a branch high up in the tree caught on another tree and gave the big maple a sudden twist. A massive lower branch swung around, knocking Amos down, and the huge trunk fell on him with a thrashing roar. He was pinned helplessly to the ground.

Amos never made a sound. His eyes were open, but he did not speak.

Solomon was stunned, frozen in horror to the spot. Then he started clawing in futile fashion at the tree trunk. He cried to his father, but there was no response. With frenzied effort, he tried to push the great cylinder of hardwood, but it did not budge.

Then, with all his might, he went to work

to cut through the large tree just above the spot where his father's body was pressed to the earth. His ax rang with rapid strokes as the chips flew. His muscles ached, but he did not feel them. His mind raced with a thousand thoughts, but he could not stop it at any one of them. When he had cut the log through he tried again to move it but it was so heavy he could not see any effect of his pushing.

He rubbed his father's hand, but it was getting cold. The look in his open eyes that stared lifelessly at the sky told even an unbelieving boy that his father was dead.

More deliberately now, he set to work to cut through the giant maple just below the point where his father's body was wedged to the ground. He was numbed with fear and grief, but his muscles worked on mechanically. Finally, he was again through the massive cylinder of wood, and then was able to roll the weight from his father's lifeless body.

For a long time he stood there looking, as the realization of what had happened slowly seeped into his being. What could he do? He must do something. Suddenly, he felt small and alone in a world that was big and cruel.

He wanted to cry, but he couldn't. He wanted to do something, but he didn't know what to do. He felt tired and sick and terribly alone.

Then he remembered Mr. Smauley and the time he had said, "If you ever need us for anything, just send the boy, and we'll give you a hand." But he could not leave his father here alone. Yet he must go for help. He tried to lift his father, but Amos was a heavy man and the boy could not move him. But he could not leave him here where wild animals might molest him. So he ran to the cabin, brought some boards, and covered the body carefully.

Then he started to run. He thought strange thoughts. He thought he was a deer with a hunter close behind. So he ran faster. He came to the trail and turned north. He knew he was tired from running, but he could not stop to rest, for some strange fear was pursuing him. His lungs ached, but his soul ached more, and he kept on. When he came to the first stream he jumped across it, his feet barely touching the few flat stones that marked the trail.

As he ran, he kept on thinking. What

should he do? The size of the problem was too great for him, but he kept on running as fast as his feet would carry him. Just running seemed to help. What would his mother say? The thought came to his mind and then dashed away again, as if it were too cruel to entertain.

The miles raced underfoot. Soon he was at the second stream and turned mechanically west. He could feel his heart pumping and his lungs ached, but, strangely, the more he ached the better he felt. With this peculiar feeling of mingled pains, he rushed into the clearing of the Smauley household.

When he saw Mrs. Smauley, another set of feelings poured over him. When he heard her voice he began to sob. He did not know what she was saying, merely that a woman's voice was saying something. He fell at her feet, and the aches and pains all came together in a rasping cry that came from deep down inside of him. He shivered and shook, and he thought he would never stop.

He could utter no words, but he could begin to hear and distinguish the words spoken around him. Mrs. Smauley was saying, "This boy is in trouble. He needs help badly. Lift him to the bed." He felt strong hands carry him to a soft place, and a warm, soft hand was placed on his forehead.

Then he heard Mr. Smauley saying, "What is it, my lad?"

But it sounded far off and unreal. He couldn't speak, and began again to shake with wracking sobs. Mrs. Smauley brought him some warm sassafras-root tea and said, "Drink this, it will make you feel better inside. Now, what is the trouble?"

He drank a little and said, "My father. He's dead."

Consoling hands touched his body, and it was good to feel other humans nearby. Before long he had told them, in brief words, what had happened.

"We must go to him at once," said Mr. Smauley. "As soon as you are rested a little we will go back."

"I am ready now," Solomon said, torn by the feeling that he should not have left at all, and the knowledge of his need for help.

In an hour the big canoe was pushing its way up the creek. Little was said as it paddled quietly along. Solomon had the feeling of being caught up in a bad dream that was making him do what he did not want to do.

When they arrived at the clearing, there was the body of his father just as he had left it. Mr. Smauley and his sons made a stretcher of their jackets and maple poles and gently carried the body to their canoe. "We'll bury him next to our Nancy," said Mr. Smauley, "if you think it is all right."

Solomon did not want to make decisions now, and, as he could not think of anything else to do, he agreed.

Mr. Smauley explained about Nancy. It was comforting to Solomon to know his father would not be alone in the burying ground. Also it made a strange bond between himself and Mr. Smauley, for he began to feel that someone else could understand his feeling and share his grief. Nancy had been twenty years old. She had wandered off into the woods one day, looking for wild flowers, and had become lost. When they found her two days later, she lay dead of fear, hunger, and exposure to the cold northern nights. Mr. Smauley explained something about death being all around but we do not always see it.

Death in particular is bad, for we lose what we value, but death in general is a part of nature and is nature's way.

Solomon was strangely comforted by Mr. Smauley's words. They helped him to feel that he was not so completely alone.

Mr. and Mrs. Smauley talked to Solomon with much kindness and tender understanding while their sons fashioned a simple wooden box and prepared a grave. The next morning, under the quiet sky, Amos Story was buried in the little burying ground. Benjamin Smauley, a deacon in the Congregational Church, read a prayer and some Psalms, and said some words about a brave and good man and a brave and good boy. Solomon heard the words as in a dream, and turned away in pain when he saw the Smauley boys reach for their shovels.

That evening, while they sat about the fireplace, Mr. Smauley said, "Solomon, we don't know what you want to do. You are a long way from the rest of your family. It would be a long trip home for a thirteen-year-old boy."

Solomon corrected him politely. "I'm fourteen now, Mr. Smauley. My birthday was in April," he said.

"That's better," continued Mr. Smauley, "but it is still a long journey for a boy your age to make alone. You can stay with us as long as you want. Maybe, with time, you can decide what you want to do."

"I know what I want to do," said Solomon. "We prepared a place for my mother and brothers and sisters. We were going to leave in a few weeks to bring them all up here. I want to go ahead just as we had planned. I know my father would want me to do it."

"If there is anything we can do to help you with your plans, just let us know," said Mrs. Smauley.

"Tomorrow I will go back to our clearing and do what needs to be done to leave it for a while. Then I will pack a few things and start home by the trail. I don't think I could handle the heavy canoe alone upstream, and we will need it here anyway. We will probably bring a pack horse all the way. We won't be able to keep it, because we don't have a barn or feed for it, but we'll work that out later." Solomon was surprised, as he listened to himself talk, for he sounded like a grownup. His training during the past few months had made him sure of himself.

I'll need a horse by fall," said Mr. Smauley. "I'll be glad to buy it from you if you decide you want to sell."

The next morning Solomon expressed his thanks for all they had done to help him in his trouble, and then he started off on a one-hundred-and-fifty-mile trek, a young, sad, but courageous head of a family of pioneers.

11. THE MESSENGER

Solomon walked into the clearing as he had done a hundred times before. He knew every foot of the land for a mile in every direction. He knew every timber in the house and every stone in the fireplace. But he felt almost like a stranger trespassing on sacred ground. It was now more than ever his home, but he had the feeling that he should not be there.

He stood for a long time at the edge of the clearing. He almost expected to hear the ring of an ax or the friendly greeting his father always gave him when he returned from any of his numerous errands. But this last errand was different. Now all was stillness, except

119

for the quiet whispering of the spring breeze in the new foliage.

Solomon looked at the last tree he had cut with his father. He felt an urge to reduce the whole tree to chips and then burn the pieces so that there would be no trace of it. He walked over toward it, saw where he had chopped through it twice, and then turned away from it. It was, after all, only a tree.

The silence in the clearing was so loud it deafened him, and he could not unscramble the noises that came to him. He knew all of the noises of the forest so well, but now it was all lost in a sound that he wanted to hear and knew he never would.

He opened the cabin door and surveyed the tasks that must be done before he started south. All of the perishable food must be destroyed. All of the food that would keep had to be made secure so that field mice, chipmunks, and squirrels would not find it.

The clothes and bedding he placed in the large chest his father had made. Then, with the broom his father had made of long turkey feathers, he swept the bare earthen floor. He fixed the table and benches so that they looked neat against the wall. He did not know at first why he was doing all these things, and then it came over him that he was getting everything ready so that when his mother came through the door she would see things just as his father had planned.

He did not want to spend the night here alone, but it was late in the day when he had finished all of the tasks he had set for himself. At dusk he set the big bolt in the cabin door from the inside, crawled out one of the windows, and wedged the shutters tightly shut. Then, with his blanket and pack, he went into the woodshed to spend the night.

The sun was not yet up when Solomon started south the next morning. He set a steady pace for himself. He would travel for about two hours and then rest for half an hour. Chunks of maple sugar made light meals but gave him energy for his trip.

The first night he stayed with settlers, and, by starting early and traveling fast, he was in Rutland on the second evening. Of course, days in May were much longer than the November days when he had last come over the trail with his father.

One of the first persons he met on the street in Rutland was the horse trader. He recognized Solomon and said, "Where is your father?"

Solomon said simply, "He is dead."

The horse trader stammered a bit, then said, "I am sorry. He was a good man."

Solomon passed on without saying anything more. He spent the night at the tavern and again was on his way early in the morning.

Day after day, he pressed on over the trail he had traveled before. His mind went back over conversations and events. Many times he lived over the happenings of the past few months, and even more times he tried to plan the words that would make the sad news more bearable for his mother.

Each night he stayed with a settler, and always he was treated with kindness. When he explained that he was going home to get his mother and brothers and sisters, he was invited to stop that way on the trip back. The people did not speak many words, but he felt their sympathy in their kind deeds.

When he came to Bennington, he was aware of great excitement in the town. He did not ask many questions, but he soon learned that Colonel Ethan Allen was expected back in town. He was to receive a hero's welcome after the brave capture of Fort Ticonderoga just two weeks before. Solomon knew that his father had thought well of Ethan Allen, and was one of his militia, though he had never been called to action. He listened to the talk along the streets, and found out that the fort had been taken without firing a shot, and even now the valuable cannon and equipment were on their way to Boston and the Colonial Army there.

Solomon did not wait to see Ethan Allen. He had more important business in Salisbury, Connecticut, so he pushed his weary feet on southward.

Eleven days after he left the clearing in Vermont, he caught sight of the church steeple in Salisbury, Connecticut. He had not looked in a mirror for a long time. He would have had some difficulty recognizing himself.

Ann Story, however, knew her son at once. She saw him come up the road, and watched with aching heart as this lonely son came toward her. He had grown tall, but he was thin, and his eyes were hollow with fatigue. His clothes were faded and torn from the long trail and hard wear. His steps were weary and dragging, as if his hurried journey were too soon over for the heavy task that now faced him.

Ann was a discerning woman. She knew Solomon would not come alone without reason. She hurried toward Solomon and drew her big boy tightly to her. Tears glistened in her eyes as she said, "Solomon, oh Solomon, tell me. Something has happened to your father."

"Yes, Mother," he said, "I'll tell you all about it. Let's go into the house."

There, in simple, direct language that she made it easy for him to use, Solomon told just what had happened. It did not seem so hard to talk now as he had thought it would be. His mother's bravery helped him. And her concern for him eased her own misery. As he talked she kept saying, "Oh, Solomon, my poor boy. What you have had to endure."

When the younger children came in from their school, they plied Solomon with endless questions, but he was tired—tired in a way he had never known before. He was weary in spirit. He had set out on a difficult mission, and he had delivered his message. Now he wanted to go off quietly and sleep, and sleep, and sleep.

Ann prepared hot soup and a large basin of hot water. Solomon ate and bathed, and then fell into a cool bed with white sheets and slept the sleep of exhaustion. The sun had been up for hours when his mother asked him if he would like breakfast.

Quickly, his strength of body and spirit returned. His mother asked him many questions, and he explained that everything was ready for her return. The cabin was built, the winter's wood stored, furniture made, and the field was planted for the fall harvest. He told in great detail about the building of the log house and of the special features of its furnishings. The more he talked, the easier it became. Yes, and the more he told about the wonders of their new home, the more anxious he was to lead them all back to it.

Solomon also told about Ethan Allen and the Green Mountain Boys, and how his father had joined the militia, first to fight the New York land claims and then to fight the

British. He mentioned also that Zeke Jenny had been seen at the trading post and was probably trapping and hunting farther north.

Ann already knew about the capture of Fort Ticonderoga. News of it had spread rapidly through the colonies and brought hope to the colonial cause. But Ann admitted that the thought of meeting Amos' old enemy, Zeke Jenny, was not pleasant.

After Solomon had had a few days of rest and renewed old acquaintances, Ann asked him about details of their proposed trip to Vermont. Solomon was pleased at the way she asked him for advice. He was no longer treated like a child but like an adult. He wondered how his mother felt about his father. She said little. He had not seen her shed a tear, except one day when he had come upon her unexpectedly and she had been sobbing with her face buried in her pillow. As soon as he appeared, however, she had dried her eyes and gone on about her household duties.

They agreed that it would be wise to go north late in August and early in September. The weather should be good for travel then, and there would be time to prepare for the winter in Vermont as well as to harvest the crops in Connecticut. Ann's younger brother was to take over the farm and make a payment each year when the crops were taken in. This would guarantee an income for Ann and her family during the years of resettlement, and, although this was never mentioned out loud, it was a place to return to if it ever became necessary.

The summer days passed rapidly. There was plenty of work for Solomon to do around the farm, but he was not satisfied. Like that first day in Vermont, when he had climbed a tree and gazed on the beautiful mountains and valley ahead, he knew that was where his heart would ever be. He wanted to be back there again.

By the middle of August, the supplies for the pack horse were prepared, and the belongings of the children were cut down to a minimum for travel. In addition to what the horse would carry, each member of the family except the two youngest would have a pack of his own.

When the time for departure came, Solomon thought of the day a year before when his father had asked him if he thought he was old enough to make the trip north with him. Now Solomon was to act as hunter, guide, and his mother's strong right arm. He wondered what another year would bring.

12. PILGRIMS' PROGRESS

Imagine, if you can, setting out on a journey of one hundred and fifty miles, into thinly settled country, with no prepared places to eat or sleep, with five children aged six, eight, ten, twelve, and fourteen. If you have taken one child on a Sunday afternoon's walk in the woods, you know of the scratches, thorns, wasp bites, and other such hazards that seem to attract children set free in a big, wide, wonderful world.

It was that kind of a world for Solomon Story, his mother, and his younger brothers and sisters, but they were not that kind of children. Of course, they could get into their share of difficulty, but they could also carry more than their share of responsibility. Hannah was six, and she took turns riding high up near the neck of the pack horse with her sister Susanna, who was eight. Samuel was ten, Ephraim was twelve, and of course, you know how old Solomon was.

The first few days of the journey were uneventful. Stops were made often, and the speed of travel was set by the short steps of the youngest members of the family. Until they reached Bennington, Ann maintained her authority, determining how far they would go and where they would stay at night.

After they left Bennington, Ann said, "Solomon, this is your country. You have been this way before. You know how far we can go and where it is safe or possible to stop. You tell us what to do."

So it was that Solomon became both guide and guard for the Story family as they moved slowly northward. He walked ahead a hundred yards or so, with his musket, and sometimes Ephraim walked with him. Ann, with her rifle over her shoulder, followed with the pack horse and the younger children.

Each day they traveled five or six miles, which was about all that the little girls could walk. It was on the third day north of Bennington, not far from where the wolves had given Solomon and his father such a troublesome night, that Solomon, walking ahead, held up his hand. There in the trail, not more than two hundred yards ahead of them, walked a black bear and a cub. They were going north also. Amos had told Solomon never to bother a bear with a cub. They were apt to be mean and vicious at such times. So the Story family followed along, almost out of sight, watching the unsuspecting bears. Once in a while the bears would sit down and scratch themselves. Finally, they shuffled off into the woods. After watching for a while to make sure the trail was safe, Solomon led the family on, but they all talked for hours about the bear and her cub.

More than three weeks had been spent in the journey when they finally came to Rutland. Ann asked humorously if the town had been named for the ruts in the road. At the tavern the family had the same room that Amos and Solomon had occupied on the first trip. Here they rested and ate well, for they knew that on the next day they would really be in the wilderness.

The next morning, when Solomon came in from some of his errands at the trading post, he found the horse trader trying to convince Ann to trade her horse for a canoe. "Its a good little horse," he said, "I'll give you a real good canoe for it." Then, as he saw Solomon walking up, he said, "Is this your boy?" When Ann nodded assent, he left suddenly, saying over his shoulder, "I knew his father, a fine man." Before Solomon had a chance to speak, the trader was gone.

Solomon had mentioned trading the horse for a canoe on the way up, but he had not told of their other dealings with the trader. Now he told the story, and the children laughed at the part where the trader was spilled in the puddle.

For the rest of the trip, Solomon planned to stay at the cabins of persons he had met and whose invitations he had remembered. The first night they came to a cabin standing just as he had seen it last, but the door was bolted tight, and the shutters were closed on the windows.

"That is strange," Solomon said. "I wonder what happened to the Fallens." He explored around the house and called, "The woodshed is open. I am sure they would let us stay there." That night they camped in the little space that was left free beside the neatly piled wood. Ann was awakened by a chipmunk scampering across her body, but, aside from that, the night was uneventful.

About noon the next day they were met on the trail by a young couple headed south. They stopped to talk. "The rangers came and told us we had better move south. The British have let the Indians loose after the capture of Fort Ti, and it isn't safe far from a blockhouse. We're going to Rutland until things quiet down. You had better come back too, with all those children."

Ann looked at Solomon, but he gave no sign of turning.

"They said nothing to us in Rutland about Indians. We have come a long way to live in a house my husband prepared for us. We do not intend to turn back," said Ann, and with that they started on up the trail.

Several of the log houses they came to were closed, but not all of the settlers had moved out. Ann and Solomon had serious talks with those who had stayed. They summed up their feelings in this way: "War is risky business. It is probably dangerous to stay on the land, but it is just as dangerous to go to some fort that the British may attack with a whole regiment. We have decided to take our chances here. The war can't last forever." Such thinking made sense, and Ann and Solomon accepted these ideas for themselves.

Two days later they again met a family traveling south. They gave the same message about Indian raids and the advice of the rangers that settlers go south until things quieted down. The family, named Pratt, said they had come down from Salisbury. When Ann said that was where they were going, they found that the Pratts had made a claim just north of the Story farm. They had arrived in June and had just finished building their cabin when they were advised to go south. "We don't mind fighting Indians," said Mr. Pratt, "but we would like some company when we are doing it."

Still, Ann and Solomon were determined to press on, and they did. Two days later, Solomon led them off the main trail and through the woods toward the clearing. For a while he was almost afraid to look, for fear the Indians had gotten there with their torches first. But, as he hurried on ahead, his anxious eyes saw the log house just as he had left it. The grass and weeds all around it were waist high, but all else was well. He pried open the shutters, climbed through the window, slid the wooden bar out of the brackets in the door, and swung it open for his mother. Then he waited to hear what she would say.

Ann asked Solomon to open the other window so that she would have more light to see the interior. Then she looked quietly around, taking in much of what had been done. Without saying anything at all, she went to the wood box, set wood in the fireplace, made a spark, and watched as the first tongue of flame began to move along the kindling. It was a symbolic act. She had started a fire burning in her new home, and she would give her wisdom and strength to see that it would not be put out.

Then she asked Solomon to unpack the horse, clear out one end of the woodshed for a temporary stall, and cut some of the tall grass with a sickle to bed down the horse.

In an hour or so she had made an inventory
of what was already in the house and added
what she had brought on this trip. She
checked the birch-bark containers for corn
meal, maple sugar, and salt. She told Solomon
she would need more containers as soon as he
could make them. These Solomon easily
made by tacking birch bark around a piece of
wood. A bit larger piece was used for a cover.

Ann said the two girls would share the big
bed with her and the three boys would sleep
in the loft above the bedroom. The boys were
set to work to gather balsam boughs for their
beds. When twilight came, the interior of the
cabin glowed with a warm and cheerful light.

The next morning Ann made a good breakfast of spider bread, made in the long-legged
frying pan. The bear grease gave it a sweet
flavor, and the coarse corn meal made it
crunch as they ate it.

Then they started the important work of
harvesting their crops. The boys were quickly
taught how to take an ear of corn and pull
back the husks and tie them. Dozens of small
branches were stuck under the rafters and the
tied ends of the corn were hung over the small
branches. So the corn was ready to dry. The

beans had dried on the vines. These were carefully picked, and the girls helped with the shelling. Some of the best corn and beans were saved to be used as seed the following spring.

Shelves in the woodshed were laden with squash and pumpkins, and some of the pumpkins were so large that the younger children could not lift them. The big green squash would last well into the winter and give many a nourishing and tasty meal.

Solomon took over as chief hunter, while Ephraim tried his fortune at fishing. Each day both boys worked hard to see who could supply more food for the table.

Ann went out into the cornfield and, with a sickle, cut and shocked the corn. As long as there was corn to eat, the horse would be satisfied.

Solomon had wondered why his mother had never expressed any opinion about the cabin and the furnishings, the land and the clearing. One night when the children were in bed, Ann sat before the fire reading her Bible. Solomon decided he would question her.

"Mother, how do you like this place?" he asked.

Ann looked from her reading into the fire, and then at her son. "I think it is the most wonderful place on the face of this earth. But what can words say about a place bought at such a price?"

13. INDIANS

Ephraim ran up from the creek, calling excitedly to his mother, "There's a man coming, there's a man coming."

A few minutes later, Benjamin Smauley walked into the clearing and called, "Halloo the house." Solomon was hunting at the time, and the girls were playing near the cabin door.

"You must be Ann Story," said Mr. Smauley. "We have been expecting you, but we thought maybe the Indian scare might have turned you back."

"Oh, Mr. Smauley," Ann said with relief, "I am so glad it is you. I want to thank you for all you did for Amos and Solomon. I heard about the roof raising and the birthday party and what you did when the accident happened. You were kind. You were a friend."

Mr. Smauley said nothing, and Ann continued. "Some persons traveling south urged us to turn back, but we could not. Our hearts are here, and we plan to stay."

"Good. We feel the same way, and because we are north of here we will help keep a lookout for you. In case of danger we will get a message to you," promised Mr. Smauley.

Just then Solomon burst in, carrying two hen turkeys he had shot. He greeted Mr. Smauley in friendly fashion and then handed him one of the turkeys. "I have found a place where they gather and I can almost always get one there. This morning I wounded two with one shot. You can have one of them for supper."

Mr. Smauley felt of the lad's muscle appraisingly and said, "We have thought of you and spoken of you many times during the last few months. You are a fine lad. Thanks for the turkey. We don't get them very often." Then after a pause he continued, "Did you tell your mother what we said about the horse last spring?"

Ann answered the question. "Yes, we have talked about it. We have no tools to use a horse with now. It is just an extra care and burden to us. We expect to get a plow in a few years. Then we would need a horse. We thought we would like to have you use the horse until we need him. He is a young horse with many years of work left in him. We'd be glad to have you use him for a while."

Mr. Smauley was pleased with the arrangement and said he would send one of the boys for the horse in a few days. He also said that he would be glad to let Ann borrow their plow and any other tools they had, if she needed them.

Ann didn't say much after Mr. Smauley left, but Solomon sensed that she felt more secure knowing there were friendly neighbors who would stop in for a visit.

In a few days, Dan Smauley came and took the horse. He had no saddle, but he put a folded blanket on the horse's back, bridled him, and rode away.

Solomon and Ephraim went to work to fill up the rest of the woodshed with split wood, for the nights were getting longer and colder, and the fire in the fireplace burned steadily.

One clear fall day, Ann was bending over the fire, preparing a stew for the noon meal, when Susanna came to her and whispered, "There are three men standing in the woods looking at us." Ann took down her rifle and moved cautiously to the doorway. She saw the men at once, and as soon as they saw her they waved in friendly fashion and started toward her. She did not put down her rifle, but she bade them come closer. They identified themselves: "We're rangers under the command of Colonel Allen. Your husband was a member of our militia. We want you to know we are sorry at what befell him. We have come to warn you of Indian danger. Indians, under the leadership of a Tory named Ezekiel Jenny, have been raiding up along the lake. They have burned the homes of many settlers. They have captured women and children. We think you should go south where it is safe."

They waited to hear what she would say. She was quiet for a while, and then said, "Won't you eat with us? I have fixed a stew made of rabbits Solomon shot."

They were all sitting around the table when Solomon walked in, empty-handed, from his hunting.

He greeted the rangers and added, "I hope Ephraim had more good fortune at the creek than I had with hunting. Everything heard me coming this morning."

Then Ann said, "The rangers want us to go south. They say that Zeke Jenny is raiding these parts, leading a pack of Indians and burning all they can get their hands on."

"What did you decide?" Solomon asked.

"I haven't decided anything yet, because I wanted you here. I've been thinking. We don't want to be foolish, and we don't want to run away. Solomon, are you still for staying?"

"Yes, Mother. I think we should stay," Solomon said. "This is our fight. We'll carry on where father left off. I never want to run from Zeke Jenny or anyone like him."

Then Ann gave her answer. Solomon would never forget it. She volunteered for service in the Green Mountain Boys, but in her own womanly way. She said, "This is our home. The father of my children prepared it for us, and this is where we belong. We want to do more than just live here. We believe in you, and we will work with you. You will need eyes and ears, and my children and I will look and listen for you. You will need shelter, and we

will have it for you. You will need food, and
we will grow and cook it for you. Give me a
place among you, and see if I am the first to
desert my post."

Solomon looked at his mother and was
proud of her. She was strong in mind and
body. She had courage. He saw what was said
of her many years later by a distinguished
judge, as a monument was dedicated to her
memory: "What her mind approved, her arm
did not tremble to execute."

After the rangers left, Ann wasted no time
in preparing for an emergency. She talked
quietly with Solomon. "Do you know of any
caves within a mile of our clearing?" she
asked. Solomon knew of none. "Then we
must make one at once," she said.

"Get the canoe ready," she ordered. "I have
an idea. The canoe leaves no footprints; if we
use it, we cannot be followed. I saw a spot that
rises sharply from the creek a short distance
from here. We might be able to make a cave
there. Let us go and see."

They found the place. Underbrush hung
low along the water's edge. Even the canoe
could be hidden securely. The roots of the
trees overhead would make a firm roof for

a cave. And the dirt that was dug out could be thrown into the water, so that there would be no telltale trace to show where the digging had been done. Ann and Solomon agreed that this would be an ideal place to build a cave. Because it was on the other side of the creek, no one would think of looking there for them.

Something about digging a cave appealed to the boyish sense of adventure in Solomon and Ephraim. They went to work with great energy at the spot Ann had pointed out. Working with their hoes, they dug a small hole in the steep surface of the creek bank, just large enough to crawl through. The dirt fell into the creek and was carried away. Beyond the opening, they made a wider space. Solomon had to make several trips back to the woodshed for the tools they needed to cut through the masses of roots. They had to dig out some large stones that were all bound up among the roots.

The two boys worked more than a week before they felt that their cave was ready for inspection. It was not quite square, and the corners were rounded. At one spot there was a stone too large for them to move, and this jutted out into the cave. The cave's greatest depth was twelve feet, and in most places it was from six to eight feet wide. It was high enough to sit up in, but only the smaller children could stand, for it was not more than four feet high in the center.

With the turkey-feather broom, they swept and swept the floor until it was quite smooth and firm. Then they brought in three canoe loads of grass which made a soft covering for the earth. They used the stone they couldn't move as a shelf. Here they stored an emergency food supply of maple sugar, dried corn, and squash. When they had it ready, they invited Ann to make a tour of inspection.

The boys were proud of their engineering feat. They helped their mother through the cave entrance, which was about three feet above the water level of the creek. She crawled in and sat down. It seemed quite dark at first, for the little light that came through the cave entrance was sifted through the overhanging bushes that were purposely left undisturbed. When her eyes became accustomed to the dim light, she said, "This should be about right. There is room for all of us. It is well hidden. We could use a couple of boards to sit on and some balsam boughs in case we need to sleep here. And when we get several persons in here it will be quite warm. You boys have done a good job."

When they were back in the cabin that evening, Ann had what she called a "council of war." Really, it was a training session for the children. Careful instructions were given about making noise. The children were told not to leave the clearing at any time, unless they had first told Ann their purpose. They were to keep their eyes and ears open at all times and report everything unusual to their mother at once.

The next morning they held a practice retreat to the cave. Each person was to carry certain items. Ann had her rifle and the tub of precious bear grease. Solomon carried his musket and a sack of meal. Ephraim carried his fishing gear and a blanket. The younger children each carried their jackets. At a given signal from Ann, each person took his appointed items and hurried through the woods to the water's edge. They climbed into the canoe and paddled quietly across and up the stream to the hidden entrance of the cave. The younger children were lifted in, with Ann following them, and Ephraim and Solomon came last, after they had secured the canoe. The whole operation took but a few minutes, and then they were all sitting safely in the dim light of their cave hideaway.

Solomon said, "Now we're ready for old Zeke Jenny and his raiding Indians."

14. FIRE

Amos' birthday came and went, and Solomon told of the details of the roof raising, as the younger children sat around the fire and gaped open-mouthed at the roof high over their heads. The days became shorter, and a few snow flurries excited the children but brought apprehension to Ann, for she knew what a long northern winter could mean.

There was hunting yet to do. Solomon had spent hours each day pursuing game through the woods, but perhaps he was too anxious. He had not shot a bear. Their supply of bear grease was low, and it was a necessity. He extended his circle of huntng farther and farther out from the clearing, but he stopped back regularly to see that all was well with Ann and the children.

One morning, early in November, he was hunting near the log house of the Pratts. It had been closed tight since they had retreated to Rutland for fear of Indians. Solomon heard noise from the clearing, as if the doors or shutters were being broken open. Cautiously, he came closer to see what was happening.

There a group of Indians, dressed in buckskin garments, were ransacking the cabin. Doors and windows were open. Noises from inside the cabin showed that they were systematically exploring the possessions of the Pratts. A white man stood quietly nearby, watching. Solomon thought this must be Zeke Jenny, though he could not be sure. He did not wait to see more. Traveling through the woods like a deer, he headed for home.

As soon as he was in the clearing, he called softly for his mother and reported to her what he had seen. As they looked north now, they could see smoke rising. They could guess that it was the home of the Pratts, set to the torch.

"Children," ordered Ann. "Take your

packs and go to the canoe. Go quietly and go fast."

Getting her rifle and an extra blanket, what little bear grease was left, and a precious kettle, Ann hurried on down the path to the creek. To say path is misleading, for Ann had warned the children to take a different way each time they went to the creek, just so there would be no easily followed path. But they took the direction to the canoe and quickly pushed out into the creek. Before they were all in the cave, they could hear noises from the clearing that told their own story.

Solomon crouched at the cave's entrance. He could see little through the protecting underbrush, but he could listen. He described to the others what he heard. There was much banging and loud noise. There were a few whoops, as the Indians expressed enthusiasm for their work of destruction. Next there was a noise like wind on a quiet night, with the crackling of fire in green wood. Then there drifted toward them the acrid odor of burning wood.

It was a sad little family that sat helplessly by while their home became charred logs and ashes. But Ann reminded them, "We are

fortunate that Solomon warned us in time to
get away to our cave. This place of hiding has
saved our lives. We can build again.''

To be safe, Ann said they would spend
the night in the cave. They had food, and it
was not too cold. They lay side by side on the
balsam boughs, fully clothed and covered
with their blankets. The cave seemed
strangely quiet. Solomon lay awake for a long
time, listening to the various noises. The children wiggled and jerked in their sleep, and
once he thought he heard quiet sobs coming
from the direction where his mother lay.

When the light of a new day began to seep
through the opening of the cave, Ann spoke
reassuringly to each child. Then she asked
Solomon to go quietly and make sure that
there were no Indians about. The Storys had
left their dwelling so quickly that the Indians
must have known there was a family around
somewhere, and they might have lain in wait.

Solomon paddled the canoe stealthily across
the creek and up the inlet. Here he made it
secure, and quietly, so quietly, stole through
the woods to the edge of the clearing. He
stood still a long time, watching for any move-

ment or sign of life, but all he saw was a few whisps of smoke rising lazily from the smoldering embers of the home he had so proudly helped to build.

The clearing was motionless. No living creature was in sight. Solomon ventured out into the clearing and toward the cabin. The fireplace and chimney stood gaunt against the leafless trees. The roof had fallen into the cabin, and all that was left of it were a few charred timbers. The walls were burned to within a foot or two of the earth. Solomon saw one of the precious hinges his father had brought from Connecticut. He started to pick it up but dropped it again instantly, for it was so hot it burned his fingers.

The table was upset. The benches were burned and broken from the weight of the timbers that had fallen in on them. A few utensils could be seen among the burned furniture.

But, standing just thirty feet away, the woodshed was not touched. Some of the bark on the side toward the cabin appeared to be singed. Evidently, the Indians had not felt it was worth bothering to burn. He pushed open the door and looked in. It was just as he had left it. He was glad, for it could again be made into their temporary dwelling.

Solomon hurried back to the cave and reported what he had seen. The younger children began to understand, for the first time, what had happened. Hannah and Susanna started to cry, and their mother rebuked them, saying, "We cry for the things we can't do anything about. Let's save our tears. We now must rebuild."

Ann and the children returned to the clearing and at once began the tasks so important for keeping a home together. She ordered the boys to stack the wood that had been in the woodshed neatly outside of it. She made a crude broom of evergreen boughs and swept out the woodshed so that it would be a clean place in which they could eat and sleep. The cave was always a second place of shelter, and they set a routine of living in the woodshed by day and the cave by night.

Solomon worked diligently, and his mind raced as fast as his feet. His blood seemed to turn hot at the thought of the cowardly men who would burn the home of a woman and her children far in the wilderness.

Finally, he spoke to his mother: "I am more sure than ever, now, that it was Zeke Jenny who set fire to our barn back in Connecticut. I never did take to the idea that wet hay could set itself on fire. Now we know what kind of a man this coward is. He would creep around in the night burning things. I am sure father would change his mind if he had seen this."

His mother reminded him that his father was usually careful about what he said, but whether it was wet hay or an angry Tory did not make too much difference when the damage was done. She continued: "You have built a cabin before. You must build us another on the same spot."

Fortunately, most of the tools had been stored in the woodshed. Solomon started as he and his father had done a year before, but, because Ephraim and his mother were not as strong as his father, he chose smaller trees. He trained Ehpraim to trim the trees as he cut them down. When they were ready to be moved, he carried one end and Ephraim and his mother carried the other end on a sapling that they put under it.

Ann spent many hours clearing out the debris which had been her home. Some treasured items were recovered. The maple sugar had run from the heat but had hardened again into queer shapes. Some of the cooking kettles were dented and blackened, but Ann scoured them with clay and soap, and they became clean again. The prized copper kettle was recovered, for it was probably too big for the Indians to carry on their journey. The bearskin rug was singed and curled into hard lumps. Ann recovered all of the hinges and the bolts that had been driven into the frames of the doors and windows. A heap of corn on the earthen floor was mixed with dirt and ashes, but Ann patiently sifted it through her fingers until nearly every grain was salvaged.

The work of rebuilding was long and slow, because double duty was demanded of each worker. Solomon cut trees part of the time and hunted to supply fresh meat for their food. Ephraim fished part of the time and trimmed the trees his brother cut. Ann helped with the building but was busy with the multiple tasks of caring for small children in a cold and uncomfortable dwelling place.

So the process continued, with days at work in the clearing and nights in the safety of the cave. Many times, Ann wondered what had happened to the Smauleys. Communication was meager on the frontier. The Smauleys had not given any warning of the Indian attack, and they had not been seen since. It was getting toward the stage in their building where they would need the help of some strong men. It was characteristic of Ann's independent spirit that she would not think of asking for help until she needed it, but now she asked Solomon if he would go to Middlebury to see if the Smauleys had escaped attack and would be willing to help them with another roof raising.

Early the next morning, Solomon started north. He needed no warning to travel with great care on the Indian trail. Now quite a different set of feelings filled his mind and heart. He was wondering about the Smauleys and what he might find there.

When he turned west at the second stream, he was prepared for almost anything but what he saw. Everything in the clearing was as usual. He was given a friendly greeting. When he told of the Indian attack and the burning of their home, Mr. Smauley was un-

able to believe it at first. He said, "The Indians must have missed us completely. We
have seen and heard nothing. We will all be
down tomorrow to work with you."

So it was that the energy of three strong
men and the companionship of a frontier
woman were added the very next day to the
rebuilding venture. Mr. Smauley and his sons
cut and notched the rafters. They split the
roof boards. After a week of concentrated
effort by the combined families, a new cabin
stood on the old foundation. Its roof was
raised, and the walls were made tight with
wood chips and clay.

Again, the Smauleys were thanked for the
part they had played in the building of the
Story cabin.

Ann and Solomon agreed that it could
never take the place of the first cabin that had
stood there. The furniture that Solomon fashioned served well enough, but it lacked the
marks of the skilled woodworker.

Christmas was near at hand. Winter would
soon set in with all its northern fury. Supplies
were badly needed to take the place of those
lost in the fire, so Ann decided to borrow the

pack horse from the Smauleys and send Solomon to Rutland. If he should be caught in a bad storm, it would be serious for him; if he did not go, it would become serious for them all. So Solomon set out, just before Christmas, to travel alone to Rutland and back.

15. RESCUE

Solomon had set off with the horse borrowed from the Smauleys. He hoped that, by starting with the first gray of the morning and riding the horse wherever possible, he would be able to cover the thirty miles or so to Rutland before dark. But the days were at their short-est, and he was not sure that he could do it. By spending a day in Rutland doing his pur-chasing, he would return on the third day. Ann felt uneasy about having her oldest son and mainstay of the home away for three days, but she tried not to show it as she wished him well when he departed.

Normal living was to be carried on in his absence. The children were assigned their daily tasks. The girls played house under their mother's feet, but she seldom lost patience. The knowledge that they were so close made her feel secure.

Ephraim was assigned the lookout toward the east, and Samuel was sent to watch along the creek. Their instructions were simple. They were to make no noise and listen for anything that sounded unusual. If they heard anything, they were not to investigate it themselves but report it at once to their mother. If they became cold they could come back to the cabin and warm themselves, but only to start out again. Thus, from the time the family came into the clearing in the morning until they left at night, they had listening posts at the edges of the clearing.

The day after Solomon left, some rangers came up the creek, and Samuel reported them well before they stepped into the clearing. He had seen their canoe before they landed it. They came to the house and asked Ann for aid. They said, "We remember what you said about being a part of us. We now need your help. We have several kegs of powder we have captured. We need them kept safe and dry

until a party comes overland to take them
south. Do you know of a safe place to keep
them?"

Ann had told no one of her cave, not even
Mr. Smauley. She had impressed on the children that no one should know of the cave, for
the secrecy of it was part of its protection. But
this was war, and she was not entitled to keep
a secret from her fighting partners, so she said,
"Yes, I have a safe place, a secret place where
we can hide the powder."

She led them to the cave, and they rolled
five small kegs of precious powder in and
stood them on the dry self of rock that the
boys had left. Then they returned to the
cabin, talking about the events of the war,
their hopes, and their fears. They told about
the Indian party that had come down from
the lake. This was the party that had burned
the Storys' cabin. It was led by British officers.
They plundered and burned, tomahawked
and scalped the few settlers who did not run
from them, and took no prisoners on their
way south. Going south, they probably did
not want to be bothered with prisoners who
might slow their progress. Before they

reached Rutland, they turned east and hit some of the settlements in the middle of the Vermont territory.

The rangers asked about Solomon. Ann told of his trip to Rutland. They said they thought the trail was free of Indians now, for they had probably returned to the lake on another one of their hunting trails. This relieved Ann, for she had thought many times of Solomon being surprised by Indians as he rode along by himself.

Before the rangers left, they told Ann the password that would be used by the men who would come for the powder. The leader would say "Boston" three times, turn completely around, and repeat the same word again three times. "It's safe to give them the powder. Take any message. We will be back," said one ranger, and they disappeared into the woods.

Ann felt like a conspirator now, as she waited for the party from the south to pick up the kegs of powder. She thought, "I can be useful. There is a reason for my staying here."

Solomon arrived on the fourth day. He had reached Rutland after dark on the first day, and started back on schedule. He was nearly back to Salisbury when he saw fresh bear tracks in the snow. He had feared that he would not get a bear before their winter hibernation. Here was a last chance, and he could not let it go. It took him hours to track the bear and shoot it. Then it took extra time to make a drag, rope the bear to it, and, using the horse, slowly drag the heavy creature the long miles up the trail to the clearing.

For a couple of days the bear was the center of interest. The fat was cooked out, the meat hung to cure, and the skin scraped for a rug to replace the one the fire had destroyed.

But this did not end the hunting tasks for Solomon. Each day, he was out early looking for fresh meat that disappeared rapidly among children who were hungry and had nothing much beside fresh meat to eat.

One morning not long after Christmas, Solomon was hunting near the Indian trail. He thought he heard a strange sound, halfway between a cry and a sob. He went toward it cautiously to investigate. He saw a woman lying near the trail. He ran at once to tell his mother what he had seen. She threw a cloak about her shoulders and, together, they hurried back through the woods. They spoke of a possible Indian plot and the dangers of ambush. They were alert and cautious. When they came near the spot, they watched, concealed, for some time before venturing close to the fallen woman.

The woman would push herself up, give a little cry, and sag down again as if fainting. When Ann and Solomon reached her, she collapsed completely. They half carried and half dragged her back into the clearing and into the warmth of the cabin.

In response to their questions, she babbled incoherently, and her eyes moved feebly in all directions, as if she could not focus them.

Ann said, "This woman is delirious from fear and exposure. And what's more, she is going to have a baby very soon."

For days Ann tended the woman with care and concern. She was fed nourishing broth and corn meal in gravy. She was massaged and kept warm near the fire. Finally, the haunting fear began to fade from her eyes, but Ann did not urge her to talk. She did not dare to move her, and each evening, when she sent Solomon and the children to the safety of the cave, she stayed behind to nurse the injured woman who could not be safely moved.

"Injured woman." That seems a strange name for a person so important in our story, but that is all we can call her. The carefully kept records that give us the names and dates of so many of the persons and events in this story never mention this woman's name or the name given to her baby. Nor do they ever tell what eventually happened to her. Like many of the persons and events of the frontier, the facts were lost in the twilight of history.

One morning, just after the beginning of the important new year of 1776, Solomon and the younger children returned to the cabin from their night in the cave to find a new person there. The new person was small but noisy. Ann was sitting by the fire trying to comfort the newborn baby. The coming of an infant to the household changed many things in the life of the Story family.

Ann had been a mother often enough so that she knew what was necessary. She did not want to neglect her own children, but the imperious demands of a new child and a new mother cannot be put aside. The common bond of danger and hardship fused the frontier people together in a family of feeling if not a family of blood relationship. Ann could no more neglect the needs of these persons than she could the needs of her own children. If she had been asked "Why?" her answer would probably not have been as clear as her action, but she knew inside her that the best insurance of life on the frontier was the concern all felt for one another.

As she became stronger, the baby's mother began to tell of her experience. She and her husband had settled east of Rutland, near one of the new communities that had sprung up there. One morning early, they were surprised by attacking Indians, with a British soldier in command. Her husband had tried to defend her and was mercilessly struck down from behind by a tomahawk-wielding Indian.

She had been taken prisoner and before long, with other captives, had been led and driven along a snow-covered trail northward. Solomon remembered the words she used to tell of her experiences: "I walked until I thought I had no strength left. Then I would fall. An Indian would drag me to my feet, and I would try again. But the weight of my child bore me down. I kept getting farther and farther behind the rest of the party. Time and again, they came back and put me on my feet, but finally they stopped coming. I don't know how long it was. And then I was here."

When the young mother was well enough to be moved, she and the baby shared the nightly trek to the safety of the cave. The baby, however, would not submit to Ann's discipline of silence. None of the children ever spoke in the cave in a voice above a whisper, but the baby did not understand the value of silence on the frontier. His high-pitched cries penetrated the stillness of both day and night. Ann and the children knew well what danger this posed for them all, but no word was said, for who could find words to tell a baby he could not cry! The presence of the woman and child was a constant reminder of the danger that was not far from any of them.

The visits of the rangers were now more frequent than they had been. They came often to see what had been heard or seen along the creek and the trail.

For some time, the fortunes of the colonies had not appeared too bright, and many persons who were loyal to the British government were trying to get north to Canada. Some bought passage on boats from the harbors of

Boston, New York, and Philadelphia, where the British were in control. Others traveled overland, and did it so well that their route was undetected.

The rangers were trying to fit together all of their bits of intelligence to see if they could fix the route of the Tories as they traveled northward, but, so far, they had had little success, and Ann and her sons could contribute little but a warm meal and a chance to take the chill out of their frost-numbed bodies.

The thought that Zeke Jenny might be one of the Tory band gave special meaning to their new task. They were working not only for the rangers but for some deep loyalty of their own to Amos' spirit. They would work as never before.

16. TORIES

It was a cold winter, and late in January the creek was frozen solid. The canoe had been pulled up onto land and covered with spruce boughs, so that it could not be recognized from a distance of a few feet.

The nightly journeys to the cave were made over the solid ice. The days were spent in the simple tasks of existence—of getting fuel for the fire and food for the body. In spite of every effort to keep the cabin warm, it seemed that the heat went up the chimney, and the cold forced itself through even the thick timbers of the log walls. Bundled in their heaviest clothes, the children were never really warm. When they stood close to the fireplace, the smell of singeing wool from one side of them did not mean that the other side was warm.

But day dragged on into day. Weeks passed by slowly, and the days began to lengthen. A February thaw broke up the solid ice in the creek. The tapping of the trees for maple sap was a welcome sign of spring to come. The sap kettle boiled day and night, and the sirup on the corn-meal mush was a treat to the taste of those who had eaten racoon, porcupine, rabbit, and turkey for weeks on end. When the sirup was poured on the snow to test it for sugar, the children grabbed up the taffylike sugar, snow and all, and ate it with delight.

Rangers came often with news. General Washington, a farmer from Virginia, had taken over the Continental Army and had laid siege to Boston where General Howe was hopelessly cornered. A call for a congress of the colonies had been sent out and would probably meet before long in an eastern city. A man named Paine was writing pamphlets telling about the cause of the colonies. These writings made emotion run high.

When the rangers came, they would pull pamphlets out of their leather boots and read to the Story family. They were brave words, and sometimes Solomon thought he should respond to the call to arms. But Ann would quietly talk to him about his responsibilities there. "There will be plenty of time for you to be a soldier when you are older. Now we need a cowshed, so that we can have a place for a cow. Milk would be good for the children, and butter would taste good on johnnycake," she said.

So it was that summer came in the year 1776 and, with it, the news of the Declaration of Independence. Solomon remembered well the August day when a single ranger stopped at the clearing. "We are a colony no longer. We are a free and independent nation. We are the United States of America."

He also gave them other information. When news of the Declaration of Independence swept through the colonies, those with loyalist feelings decided that this was not a mere skirmish among disgruntled colonists, but a war to the finish. They decided that now was the time for them to hurry to Canada and safety. Many were going there to enlist in the King's army to fight against the newly formed government.

The rangers said: "We are watching the trails. We need all the information we can get. These people are dangerous. They are fanatical in their loyalty. British agents are coming down into the colonies to lead the Tories north. We warn you to beware of them. If you have a place to hide, you had better do it."

So Ann decided to again use the cave at night.

During daylight hours, gardening, hunting, and the numerous household tasks had to be done. The added needs of a mother and baby kept Ann busy from dawn until dusk.

A rude cowshed appeared in the clearing. Solomon thought large, and so he built large. There would be room for a cow and a calf, and maybe another cow, in time. Overhead was a place to store hay as well as a place for children to play on a rainy day.

At night, the family went to the cave. Such is the nature of history that big things often hinge on little things. So it was that an important chapter in the history of the Green Mountain Boys rested on the unexpected cry of a baby in the dark of the night.

The loyalty and service of Ann Story to the cause of freedom were well known, not only to the rangers but to their enemies. One of these enemies was a British agent who posed as an uninterested hunter, but who was a special person to the Story family. He traveled these frontiers of the no man's land between the colonies and Canada with a purpose. He was one who led the loyalists north through the valleys and mountains to Canada. Secretly, he carried enlistment papers for the army of General Burgoyne.

This British agent, Ezekiel Jenny, or Zeke, as the Storys knew him, was leading a group of Tories toward their rendezvous on the shore of Lake Champlain. They had learned to hide by day and travel by night to escape the watchful eyes of the rangers, who knew these hills and valleys as they knew their own farms. Stealthily, they made their way along a trail of their own. They did not follow the known trails that would be watched. They avoided the paths that others took, for, if they were captured, they would be treated either as spies or as traitors. At best, they would be imprisoned, and they might well be shot. So their caution was warranted.

As they crept along through the moonlight, Zeke Jenny followed the west bank of Otter

Creek. He was startled to hear the sharp sound of a baby's cry coming from almost directly under his feet. He thought he knew what it was. He, at last, had found the hiding place of that troublesome Ann Story who had caused him and the other enemies of the colonies so much grief by the accurate information she gave to the rangers.

Sending the rest of his company ahead, he sat down quietly to wait for the appearance of Ann Story. When the light of morning came, he heard a rustling in the underbrush, and, a few seconds later, a canoe filled with women and children moved slowly out into the stream.

"Halt!" he yelled, and aimed his rifle directly at Ann. "At last I've got you," he gloated.

But who can call halt to a stream as it flows? "Pull that canoe into shore," he ordered, and Ann told Solomon and Ephraim, who manned the paddles, to comply.

"Now get out," he ordered, and Ann stepped ashore with the baby in her arms, as the others watched fearfully. The boys held tight to some branches to keep the canoe from moving along with the current.

"Now talk," Jenny ordered, as he tried to terrorize her with his gun held close to her chest. "Tell me where I can find the hide-out of the Green Mountain Boys. Don't try to bluff me. I know you know. Tell me, or I'll blow your heart out."

Ann gave him no true information. Instead, she gave evasive and meaningless answers. This made Zeke Jenny angry, and he threatened to shoot her on the spot if he did not get the information he wanted. "I can treat you like a spy," he said.

Still she looked at him defiantly and said, "I dare you to shoot a defenseless woman in cold blood. You are too much of a coward to pull the trigger. Now go, for the very sight of you makes me sick."

Her clear, cool gaze wilted his bluster. He did not know what to do next. Finally, he lowered his gun and backed away with nothing better than this to say: "You'll live to regret this day. I'm telling you now."

Slowly, he backed for a distance down the stream as if he dared not turn his back on Ann's defiance. Then he turned and trotted out of sight.

Immediately, Ann was again in the canoe

and across the stream. She went to the cabin, wrote a brief note on the back page of her Bible, tore out the page, and handed it to Solomon, saying, "Go as fast as you can to Ned Hatch, the ranger." And Solomon was gone.

That night the unsuspecting Tories thought they were safely beyond the last of the frontier settlements. They boldly built their campfires and talked freely of their escape from the rebellious colonies. Little did they realize that the encounter of Zeke Jenny with Ann Story had put them all in danger. Even then, their camp was surrounded by Green Mountain Boys, waiting for the signal to open fire.

Hour by hour they waited, as more and more reinforcements came in response to the system of signals that the rangers used. Then, as the light of the campfires began to fade and the campers slept, the hoot-owl signal echoed through the stillness of the night.

Instantly, the night roared aloud with musket fire, and the woods rang with the shouts of the rangers. The startled sleepers awoke in bewilderment, and soon were surrendering to their captors who emerged from the darkness. The shots had been fired in the air, for the rangers meant no physical injury to their captives if they did not resist.

Soon the Tories and their leaders were herded together, their weapons distributed among their captors. Over a hundred men who had already signed enlistment papers with General Burgoyne's agent were on their way south to imprisonment. They would not take arms against their fellow colonists. They would not have a chance to destroy the cause of freedom.

So it was that the cry of a baby in the night, and the events that followed upon it so quickly, broke the back of a secret movement by which hundreds of persons unfaithful to the cause of freedom would have shouldered arms against their former neighbors.

This action brought an end to British and Indian excursions along the Vermont part of the northern frontier. Settlers began to come back to the clearings they had left in fear. A new feeling of stability and security came with them. Ann and her family had won for themselves a place of honor on the frontier. Ann wanted no praise. She believed in a cause. She had worked and suffered for it. The prospering of the cause was its own reward.

But Ann Story would gladly have admitted that she felt a deep satisfaction to know that she had contributed directly to the capture of an enemy of her husband as well as an enemy of her country. She could be more comfortable now that she knew Zeke Jenny would no longer be leading Indians south and Tories north.

17. A BOY BECOMES A MAN

Early in the fall a settler traveling north brought a letter for Ann from her brother. It carried a payment for her share of the summer's crop in Connecticut. This would buy a cow.

Again, Solomon was given the task of doing the buying. He had built the cowshed. He had helped fill its loft with hay. Now he could have the privilege of buying the cow and leading it home.

Rutland was the nearest place for such a purchase, so Solomon set out again for the trading center many miles away. But travel was different now. The cabins that had been closed were occupied. New life had come to the frontier.

This new life was evident at Rutland. A crier at the entrance to the tavern called out every hour the terms of enlistment in the army of George Washington. Every hour, Solomon went to listen. The small groups that stood around talked much about the war and the army. He heard that there was a promise of land in payment to soldiers when the war was over. He heard that the property of the Tories was being sold and the proceeds were being divided among the soldiers. He was so filled with thoughts of war and the advantages of enlistment that, at times, he forgot about the cow he had come to buy.

He made inquiry at the trade post and found where there was a cow for sale. He was looking for a young cow that had just had a calf. His mother had given him money to buy the cow, and had told him that he could use the balance to buy whatever he thought they needed most. He had found out in the trading post that a shipment of glass had recently come from Bennington. He thought the cabin needed glass for its windows more than anything else, and he was determined to buy the cow and the glass for the amount of money his mother had given him.

When he saw the cow that was for sale by one of the local farmers, he knew at once that it was just what he wanted, but it took much talking to get the farmer to sell it for the price Solomon would pay. But the deal was made, and the glass was bought. The cow made a strange-looking pack animal as it wandered slowly along the trail, carrying the bundles of glass hung over its back.

Ann and the children welcomed Solomon and the cow. The cow was soon almost a member of the family. Ann did the milking, but all enjoyed the milk and butter. With a cow on their farm, life was making a long step toward becoming civilized.

Solomon said nothing about the recruiter and his hourly cry before the tavern in Rutland, for he remembered what his mother had said the last time he had talked about enlisting. Also, he knew from his inquiries that he was not old enough. He would not be sixteen until the next April.

But the whole subject was brought up one

day when Mr. Smauley stopped for a visit. He appraised the cow and said he thought Solomon had made a good purchase. Then he said that his sons, Dan and Eli, had signed up and were going to serve with General Washington and his Continental Army. Ann looked knowingly at Solomon, and, though she said nothing, he thought he saw in the look of understanding she gave him the attitude that would make it easier for him to talk with her about his feelings when the day came.

During the summer the Story family tended its crops well, and the harvest was good. Bushels of dried beans were stored in the sleeping loft. Bags of nuts were gathered and stored. Hundreds of ears of Indian corn hung from the rafters. The sleeping loft, the woodshed, and even the cowshed were piled high with pumpkins and large squash. With the milk from the cow, Ann knew that her family would not be hungry during the winter months.

Butter was a regular part of the family diet now, and some sour cream had been cured for a tasty cheese.

The glass that Solomon had bought was
fitted into a well-made frame, and it let so
much light into the cabin that it became a
much more cheerful place in which to live.

When Mr. Smauley brought them a puppy
one day, Ann was at first hesitant about keeping it, but the children fell in love with it at
once, and she could not deny their pleas for a
pet. Then too, as Mr. Smauley said, "What is
a farm without a dog?"

Ephraim was growing to be a tall, strong
lad. He was older now than Solomon had been
when he first came north with his father.
Without saying why, Solomon was careful to
teach Ephraim everything he knew about
hunting, farming, and woodcraft. Ephraim
was a ready pupil and worked well with the
older brother he idolized.

The second winter that the Story family
spent in their log house was far more pleasant, though less eventful, than the previous
one. There were no fires, no Indians, and
no weary captives to rescue. No babies were
born, and no nights were spent in the
cramped quarters of the cave hiding place.
More neighbors were at hand, and there was

friendly visiting back and forth. Life assumed a far more normal and even rhythm, and the fearful loneliness was banished.

The rangers came less often, for most of them had been sent closer to the concentrations of British troops. General Howe had been forced to board ship with his soldiers and leave Boston to the colonial troops. This was considered to be a great victory for the colonists.

When the rangers did come, they brought newspapers and pamphlets. These they read aloud and then folded into their boots to read again to the next settlers they visited. And each time they went, Solomon had a feeling of uneasiness. He never knew quite what it was, and, if asked, he probably could not have given a clear description of how he felt. Perhaps it was that he felt so far away from the important events that were making history in the new nation.

He was in Rutland, buying more tools and clothing for the family, on the first birthday of the new republic. He shared much of the enthusiasm and the bold talk of those who told what they thought would happen to the British who were even then invading New York from the north.

He had been back in Salisbury but a few weeks when Mr. Smauley visited them and reported the glorious news of the battle at Bennington. All of Vermont was overjoyed at the story of what happened to the Hessian invaders who had sought to steal horses and cattle from the settlers in the southern part of the state. They went reeling backward into New York, not only defeated but leaving behind their valuable cannon and other supplies.

Mr. Smauley said that now Army recruiters were going out through the settlements to enlist every able-bodied man and boy for what they all knew must be a decisive engagement when General Burgoyne finally met the main part of the American Army.

Ann said nothing, but she had been watching Solomon's increasing restlessness as he went about his tasks. A part of him was far away. He spent hours polishing and adjusting his musket so that it was in perfect working order.

It was no surprise to Ann when a recruiter

stopped at the clearing one day. He explained that the battle of Bennington was but the beginning of a major battle for possession of New York State and the Hudson River Valley. He explained the British plan to divide the colonies from New York City to Canada. This was the strategic moment, and now was the time when men were needed more than ever before.

The recruiter asked Solomon if he would like to sign the papers. Solomon looked at his mother questioningly. Before she said anything, he reminded her, "I was sixteen in April. I am old enough to sign up. Ephraim is now older than I was when I led you back to this place and helped you get settled. Things are safer here now, and you have more food and closer neighbors than we had then. I have had training in the woods and with my musket. I think I am needed now at the battle front more than I am here."

Ann listened to these words and was proud of them. Her mind raced back over the events that had made her boy a man ahead of his years. She had put a man's responsibility on his young shoulders. She could not now take back what she had so freely given. She had wanted him to be a man; now she must value his manhood.

Her mind pictured again the tired boy who had trudged into Salisbury two years before. He had grown strong and handsome since then. She had sent him off on dangerous journeys, expecting him to act like a man. And he had. Now she fought her mother's inclination to see only the boy in him.

This is what she said: "I have raised you to value freedom. I have trained you to accept responsibility. I knew you would become a good man. I did not know it would come so soon, but I cannot stand in the way of it. You are right. We will do well here, and you are needed there."

The enlistment papers were quickly signed, and Solomon packed at once to leave with the recruiter. The farewells were firmly said, as strong people say them.

When Ann embraced her tall son she said quietly, "God bless you and keep you, my son. Remember, this is always your home, and we are always your people."

She watched him to the edge of the clearing, as he strode off to that engagement that historians have called one of the fifteen decisive battles of history, the Battle of Saratoga.

But in her mind she was saying, "I gave my husband to this new country. I made a man of a boy too soon. Must I give him too?"

And she turned her face toward the wall.

EPILOGUE

For a number of years there is no record of
Solomon Story and his adventures. The records of the war years were, in many instances,
poorly kept, and often, if kept, were later lost
or burned.

We do know that Solomon returned from
the war, for his name appears on the tax lists
of Salisbury as an independent landowner
within five years after the war was over and
just after the Constitution of the new republic was ratified.

Ann raised all her children to healthy manhood and womanhood. She herself lived to
ripe years and often described to her children
and grandchildren, in modest fashion, the

events that occupied her early years in Vermont.

Fifty years ago her memory was honored with a monument at West Salisbury, Vermont, at the exact place where the Story cabin was built and rebuilt.

On the monument were written these words: "Ann Story, In Grateful Memory of Her Service in the Struggle of the Green Mountain Boys for Independence." So much for the woman who was called, "The Mother of the Green Mountain Boys."

I trust that the words in these pages will serve as a living monument to a teen-aged boy who shared her fortunes and also deserves the praise.

Chelsea, Vermont   August, 1961